MARKS OF MENACE

With the mysterious mute girl guiding him, young Isar traveled cautiously through the countryside, ever farther from the protection of the Temple of the Sun, ever deeper into the dark unknown.

He passed by overgrown fields, devastated cottages, abandoned villages. Then he began to meet the survivors, their eyes blank, their movements puppetlike. On their foreheads he saw the still-festering wounds that marked them as slaves to the monstrous new masters of the land.

Isar had been trained in the arts of magic. But no training could prepare him for the force he was about to struggle desperately against . . . as even the miraculous power of the sun dimmed before the thickening clouds of chaos and the rising storm of horror . . .

SHADOW ON THE STONES

SHADOW ON
THE STONES

Moyra Caldecott

FAWCETT POPULAR LIBRARY • NEW YORK

SHADOW ON THE STONES

Published by Fawcett Popular Library, a unit of CBS Publications, the Consumer Publishing Division of CBS Inc., by arrangement with Hill and Wang, a division of Farrar, Straus and Giroux.

ISBN: 0-445-04502-7

Printed in the United States of America

First Fawcett Popular Library printing: January 1980

10 9 8 7 6 5 4 3 2 1

*For my family
with love*

The Messenger

The traveller was exhausted. It had been many days and nights since he had eaten or had rested. His clothes were torn, his body filthy and his eyes wild and red. He knew that if he followed the ancient customs it might be a long time before he received an audience with the High Priest. There was no time left for such formality.

He had heard good reports of the dark Stranger Priest from over the sea and knew that his wife, the Lady Kyra, was noted not only for her exceptional powers as priest and Lord of the Sun, but for her sympathy and understanding of all who came to her in trouble. He knew also that she was of his own land, and no stranger to its problems.

It was not easy to find his way within the maze of wooden priest-houses and long student huts that clustered closely around the great Temple of the Sun, but he was desperate to deliver his message and his desperation gave him courage to dodge and hide. He came at last to the High Priest's home, set back among trees and separated from the others, but otherwise hardly distinguishable from them, and not of the grandeur he would have expected.

There was no marker of crossed feathers above the skins that hung over the doorway, to indicate that entry was not permitted, and indeed they were drawn aside and fastened so that the cool air and the light could pass into the interior.

He crossed the threshold swiftly before he could be seen or stopped.

"My Lord, I must speak with you," he cried in a voice breaking with weariness and urgency, and then almost stumbled and fell at the contrast between the vibrancy of the light in the outside world and the inner, still, darkness of the chamber.

He could see nothing.

Watching him in some alarm stood Deva, now thirteen summers old, alone in her mother's chamber, dressed in her mother's robes, her face painted with ceremonial paint, the crown of the Priestess upon her head. She knew that she was not allowed to wear this even in play, but there had been no one to see her and the temptation to try it on had been too great.

Frightened, she stared at the rough, uncouth intruder. Was he human robber or demon drawn to her from the hidden realms by the sacrilege she had just committed?

To the man standing in the doorway, his eyes gradually adjusting to the dim light within the house, she was a priestess in full regalia, standing impassively and calmly, waiting for him to deliver his message.

"My lady," he said softly, stumbling forward a few steps to fall on his knees before her.

"I beseech you . . ." he continued in a low voice. He found himself trembling and the words catching in his throat.

He had thought about this meeting many, many times as he had travelled the long, weary way from his home in the west country, but never had he imagined he would feel such awe in the presence of another human being. This must be the great Kyra, the Lady who had repelled an army with power from her slender hand. She was looking at him now with dark eyes, eyes as bright as jet, and the words he had rehearsed so many times would not come to his tongue.

She did not move.

"My lady," he tried again at last. "Forgive me that I break in upon your home . . . that I come to you with no preparation, no ceremony . . . forgive me . . . my appearance . . . I would not have had it so, but the matters that I would bring to your attention are urgent beyond all ceremony, all appearance . . ."

His voice trailed away. She was so beautiful and there was a scent so strong and so holy about her that he could hardly bear it.

He dropped his eyes from her black gaze and stared helplessly at the point where her long cloak of white and blue touched the ground.

It would be easier to talk to the High Priest, her husband. He had never been at ease with beautiful women, and this one was beautiful beyond any he had ever seen.

Meanwhile Deva in her borrowed robes was puzzling what to do. She knew she should acquaint the man at once with his mistake and lead him to her mother, but . . . and here the little thread of mischief in her gave a tug . . . she was enjoying the role of priestess and she saw no harm in playing it a moment or two longer.

She raised her hand with a graceful and imposing gesture.

"Rise," she said as imperiously as she could. "There is no need to kneel to me."

At least that was no lie, Deva told herself.

"My lady," the man almost crawled forward. "May I touch your hand?"

Deva found herself lowering it to him grandly, flushing slightly at the thrill of power she felt stirring within her.

Instead of touching her fingers briefly as she had thought he would, he seized her hand and started covering it with kisses, tears streaming from his eyes and down his rough and dusty face.

Fear and pleasure fought for control over her. She was at once horrified at herself for allowing this to happen, and for enjoying it.

She pulled back her hand sharply.

The man gave a kind of sob and fell fainting at her feet.

Terrified, she stared at him.

She thought she would remember until the end of her days the tears in his eyes when he thought he was kissing the hand of the legendary Kyra. The story of Kyra's part in Panora's War had spread throughout the land and was sung by many a poet on feast days. She had become worshipped almost as though she were a god. Indeed Deva had heard her mother complaining about this to her husband, the Lord Khu-ren, and protesting that it was wrong for anyone to set her aside so from other people. Her powers were no greater than his or those of the former High Priest, the Lord Guiron. Together they had tricked the enemy into defeat, using what skill they had as human beings trained to work with the Spirit Realms, the Lords of Light.

Her mother would not have allowed the man to grovel so, and Deva felt tears of shame in her own eyes for her part in the embarrassing scene.

With shaking hands she lifted the crown of the priestess off her head and struggled to unpin the robes about her shoulders. She was determined to be out of the clothes before anyone else saw her. Her mind was racing with thoughts of how she could undo the harm that she had done.

As soon as she was clad once more in her own tunic, she reached to fetch water for the man, spilling it from the earthenware beaker in her haste.

His eyes opened and he stared bewildered at the dark haired girl child leaning over him.

He shook his wet hair free from the water she had poured upon it, and dragged himself in confusion to his feet, gazing around himself, only half remembering what had occurred.

"You must have had a vision," the girl was saying breathlessly. "A dream . . . a vision . . ." she gabbled, "you fainted . . . you are better now!"

"My lady . . ." the man murmured, looking around the chamber, thinking of the stately priestess he had seen with gold upon her head.

"No, she is not here. You had a vision," Deva insisted, her heart cold with the lie she was telling, and yet still telling it.

The man was silent.

He was tired, so tired he feared he might not be able to keep upright much longer.

"I must . . ." he said at last, painfully, pulling the words out of an aching body. "I must see her . . . I need . . . we need . . . help . . ."

"You will have it!" promised Deva hastily. "Just do not fall down again."

She pulled his arm and seated him upon a wooden bench.

She thrust a beaker full of water into his hands.

"Drink that," she said with a semblance of control returning to her voice. "I will fetch the Lady. Do not fall!" she added commandingly as he swayed.

He forced himself to remain upright.

"Hurry . . ." he whispered.

But she was already gone.

He saw the skins at the doorway still moving from the touch of her shoulder.

He thought it was a breeze that made him feel so cold and every moment colder.

When an agitated Deva returned with her mother they found him lying on the floor, the earthernware beaker smashed to pieces beside him and the spilled water already seeping into the clay floor.

"O no," cried Deva, "he has fainted again!"

She rushed for more water as Kyra kneeled beside him.

When she returned her mother was standing very tall and still beside the figure on the floor.

She lifted her hand to stop her daughter approaching any nearer.

"He is dead," she said quietly.

Deva stood stunned.

She herself was near to fainting with the shock.

What had she done?

She had deceived a dying man and wasted precious moments in foolery when they were the only ones he had.

Kyra straightened the stranger's dusty, crumpled body and asked Deva to join her in lifting him to lie with greater dignity upon the soft rush bed.

The girl shuddered as she touched his cold skin.

"What will we do, my lady?" she whispered. "He asked for help but we know nothing of the nature of the help he wanted."

Kyra was deep in thought.

"Leave us," she said to Deva.

As Deva withdrew Kyra sat quietly down beside the
stranger, the stone sea urchin that was for her a talisman of power in one hand, the other upon his forehead.

There was no way she could call him back from the
dead, he was not a priest who knew how to die in
stages and with control, but a rough man of action who
had fallen into death unwillingly and unprepared. Her
only chance was to draw from the air around him the
last vibrations of his thoughts before they moved beyond her reach on to another level of reality.

The Shadow of Fear

Isar made camp in a small cleft between two hills. It would perhaps have been more sensible if he had chosen a position nearer the top of the hill where the view of the surrounding countryside would have given him warning of any approaching danger, but he foresaw no danger.

A spring bubbled from lichen-covered rock and the green fronds of ferns enclosed the place as though it were enchanted.

He set his fire carefully so as to disturb the harmony of the place as little as possible and the scent of wood smoke rising through tall trees and leaning bushes tugged gently at his memory of other places and other times that had been so wreathed in peace and quietness that they had become special times, times that brought renewal and refreshment.

He enjoyed being alone and never felt lonely. In the silence amongst growing things he had often felt the subtle stirrings of communication between all that existed and himself. This was a gift his mother, Fern, had given him for a birth present as other mothers give sun-metal or moon-metal discs. Growing plants did not speak to him quite as they did to her, but his sense of vision was more than ordinarily developed and an arrangement of leaf and twig that would pass unnoticed by others could be a potent source of joy and revelation to him.

No one knowing Isar would associate him with his natural father, the cruel magician Wardyke. He had all his mother's features and qualities. He was slender and lithe, his hair the colour of copper, his face gentle, his eyes light hazel with flecks of gold. His tallness might be inherited from Wardyke, but that was all. The Spear-lord Karne had brought him up as his own son, and it was Karne he respected as his father since Wardyke's death.

He was sitting now with his back against a rock, relaxed and sleepy, watching the night shadows gradually snuffing out the distinctive patternings around him, pleased by the graceful and sinuous dance of the thin thread of smoke from his small fire, when he fancied he saw a shadowy figure standing in the darkness behind the smoke. So tenuous was the impression that he narrowed his eyes to afford a better focus, but did not move a limb in case the disturbance either dispelled the vision (if it were a vision) or caused the animal to charge (if it were an animal).

As he stared and his eyes began to smart with staring, he began to "feel" that it was Deva.

His ordinary senses gave him no evidence of this, but he began to have the feelings in himself that he always had when Deva was near, stirrings of happiness and warmth, protectiveness, and also, sometimes, a touch of amused irritation.

But now he felt that she was worried and afraid. She seemed to be weeping and reaching out to him.

Forgetting momentarily where he was, he moved to take her in his arms, but even as he did so he realized that she was not there and it was the night held at bay by the last flickering of his fire, that waited under the trees.

In the morning, after a restless night of bad dreams he could not remember when he woke, he decided to return home. The impression he had received of Deva in trouble had been strong, even though it had been indistinct. He was determined to find out more about it even if it did mean he would not meet Janak, the great man he was travelling to meet, the man who could make dead wood live again in new forms.

As he packed his few belongings in to the leather pouch he carried slung over his shoulder, and returned the ashes of his fire with gratitude to the forest from which they had come, he argued with himself about his decision. He knew Deva would have tried to stop him had she known that he was leaving upon such a long

journey, however innocent, and it was for this reason
that he had not told her of it himself. He knew she was
spoilt in many ways and had innumerable tricks to
twist events the way she wanted them. By now she
would have found him gone and would be wanting him
at her side again to torment and delight. As the daughter of two priests it would not surprise him if she had
ways of reaching him not available to ordinary people.

And yet . . . and yet there was something more to
her pain this time . . . something deeper . . . more urgent . . . more serious.

He would turn back.

As he reached the top of the easternmost of the two hills
that had sheltered him in the night, the one he had
climbed down to find his camping place, he took a last
yearning look to the west.

On the horizon he could see a dark and ominous
cloud of smoke. At first he thought it might be an ac-
cumulation of cooking fires and was about to turn
away, when something made him stay.

He was never afterwards sure whether it was the
scent of fear in the air, the sense of someone standing
beside him pointing to the smoke, instantly gone as he
turned his head, or curiosity within himself, that made
him travel towards the west and not the east that day,
forgetting Deva.

He journeyed far into the day before he neared the
place where the fire had been. The smoke had died

down long before he reached it but he had marked its position in relation to rocky outcrops and free-standing trees, and thus had no difficulty in finding it.

Several times he saw groups of strangers carrying weapons and an instinct made him avoid them. He had never been as far west as this before, but the descriptions he had had of the gentle people who lived in the country did not tally with those he saw. In each case the sound of their voices, talking in an unknown tongue, was aggressive and harsh. But it was only when he saw one shoot a bird and laugh to see it fall, drawing his arrow callously from the broken feathered body, that he knew for sure these were not his people.

He took greater care in his journeying, keeping to the bushes and the trees, avoiding open places, his heart heavy and anxious.

When he caught sight of the silhouettes of a group of Tall Stones upon a rise of ground his spirits leapt. Here at last would be the real people of Klad, the people who worshipped the Lord of All, symbolized by the burning disc of the Sun and the Sacred Circle of Stones.

Although he was tired, his pace quickened and he ran the last part of the way.

Where there was a Circle there would be a Priest and a village community. He would settle at last the questions that tugged and scratched at his mind.

But as he came within clearer sight of the Stones he went cold.

This was not as it should be.

The whole area was blackened and charred by fire. The village that had been sprawling comfortably around the base of the knoll was now no more than smouldering embers and a broken cooking pot or two.

There was no sign of life and the air carried an acrid stench and a dry warning of hurt and danger.

He turned to the Stones and nausea and horror overcame him.

The beautiful Circle that had stood since ancient times for communion amongst all the Realms of Being was desecrated beyond belief and seemed to crouch like a wounded and despairing animal waiting for death.

Slowly Isar's eyes moved from Stone to Stone and at every one he saw the burnt and mutilated body of a man, in some cases the hide ropes that had bound them to the Stones not quite burned through.

Their pain was still present and he fell to the ground with the weight of it.

"O God," he sobbed, "O Lord of All that Is! How *could* you let this happen?"

A small breeze drily stirred the ashes.

No answer came to him from the blind Circle of Stones.

After this . . . long after this . . . he gathered himself together and turned back towards the east.

Now he would go home.

He would walk through the night.

He would not rest until he had left the pain and evil he felt in this place far, far behind.

Night creatures called shrilly from the darkness.

Moonlight drew grotesque shadows from the trees.

Twigs cracked where no one walked.

The world that had enclosed him up to now with such loving care, had turned hostile.

At the dawn he found himself further west into the land of Klad than he had been the evening before, and no matter how fervently he wished it, he could make no progress towards the east.

It was a long time before he came upon a village that was inhabited.

He paused upon a neighbouring hill and watched it closely before he approached.

He longed for friendly human contact and a warm and comfortable place to sleep, but caution held him to his post and he lay still, marking all who came and went with close attention.

The village itself seemed unremarkable enough, a cluster of small homesteads of wood and turf, smoke from cooking fires rising steadily, the cattle and sheep driven to their separate enclosures of banked earth and thorn-brake by village lads. He saw girls drawing water from the stream and carrying it in leather bags and earthenware pots as in his own village. If he had not seen what he had seen, nor sensed the menace in the air, he might not have noticed that all he saw were moving sluggishly like a stream choked by weed in time of drought. Even the young girls carrying the water had no spring to their walk and instead of chattering and calling to the boys as girls in his own village used to do, they kept silent, with eyes down, and there was no whistling with the cattle drive or singing amongst the shepherd boys.

He moved closer, every sense alert. He noted heaviness of heart, slowness, inertia, lack of any kind of hope or will to live, but there seemed to be no immediate danger.

He looked at the sky and knew that heavy rain was very close.

He decided to trust the village and, light as a deer attuned to danger, he sprang down the hillside, scarcely dislodging a pebble from its resting place.

He stopped at the edge of the village, facing an old man milking a cow.

As soon as the man became aware of Isar's presence, he stiffened as though expecting some harm to come to him, not believing that there was any way to avert it. He stopped his milking and stood up, arms hanging limply at his sides, head bowed, waiting.

Isar stared at him.

It seemed that he, Isar, was the one to be feared.

He noticed that the man had an ugly sore at the centre of his forehead, but otherwise, apart from his weary docility, was not unlike a number of old men Isar had seen in his own community.

Isar waited for the customary greeting of host to traveller, but it was not forthcoming.

He was plainly expected to say the first words and, although it made him uncomfortable so to break with tradition, he felt obliged to do it.

"I greet you, sir," he said gently, "and may the Spirit Helpers of the Lord Sun be with you, teach you their ways and keep you from harm."

The age-old form of words that Isar had used so often as greeting that they had become commonplace to him, seemed to shatter the mood of waiting resignation in the man.

He looked up startled, his eyes instantly going to Isar's forehead as though seeking something there, and being surprised that he did not find it.

The man was plainly confused, not knowing whether to return Isar's greeting or to run for cover.

Isar slowly raised his hand in the salute to the Sun his mother had taught him before she had taught him to speak.

Fear in the man's face began to give way to hope.

He opened his mouth, but no words would come.

Slowly, tentatively, he raised his own hand in answer, and then in terror looked around to see if it had been observed.

"Do not fear me," Isar said, "I am a traveller. I know nothing of this land or what it is you fear. I seek only lodging for the night."

Other villagers joined them, and stood behind the man, staring at Isar. His eyes went to their faces, seeking the one who was their Priest or Elder and who would speak for them without the fear the rest so plainly showed.

On each face, on each forehead, in the centre, was a sore still festering, or a scar that bore witness to a sore that had once been there.

His hand went involuntarily to his own forehead and he felt the smooth skin with relief, momentarily experiencing a twinge of fear that the mysterious power that seemed to hold this people subject had pierced his own forehead in some way since he had entered its realm.

The villagers watched him warily.

The man he had greeted turned to them and spoke at last.

"He used the old greeting," he said with awe. "He is not one of Them, nor of Us. He is a traveller."

The villagers moved closer, still wary, but their curiosity and the dawning of hope in their hearts driving them on.

"Where are you from, traveller?" The old man asked.

"From the east, from Haylken, the Temple of the Sun."

"Groth?" The man said.

Isar looked puzzled. He did not understand the word.

The blankness on his face worked on the people like rain on a parched land.

Suddenly there was movement and sound.

He was seized and bustled and jostled until he found himself in a small and crowded house. Some of the people had pushed in with him, but the rest had scattered like frightened birds from a farmer's field-strip when the farmer's son shouts and bangs sticks together.

The old man he had first approached seemed to be the one most in charge. Silent as the people had been before, now questions poured from them and their eagerness to hear his answers pulled him from side to side until he was dizzy.

"How did you escape from the burning?"

"How is it that the guards did not see you?"

"Are you from the Temple itself?"

"Were you sent?"

"Do they know that we need help?"

"Are they coming to help us?"

They touched him. They kissed him. Time and again hands stretched to his forehead and trembling fingers felt the smoothness of his brow.

"Stop, stop!" He called at last. "I cannot answer all your questions until I have asked you some of my own."

"Ask!" They cried, eager now to communicate in any way possible.

They knew he was from the east.

They knew he did not understand the dread word Groth.

"Why is it that you all have wounds upon your foreheads?"

"It is the Mark," they said, "the Mark of Groth. We are slaves of Groth."

"This word 'Groth'—what does it mean?"

The daring of his question silenced them for an instant and then they all tried to talk at once.

"No," he laughed, holding up his hands to fend off the confused and flying words. "One at a time. I have not as many ears as you have voices!"

They looked at each other.

The old man Isar had first encountered, whose name he learned was Keel, was tacitly chosen to be their spokesman.

"He is the new god," he said, and his voice carried fear even at his daring to speak the words so, without reverence.

Isar looked amazed and sceptical.

"How can there be a *new* god?" he said scornfully. "God has been from Always. There is no Before and no After."

"Ah yes," Keel lowered his voice and he spoke in the way a man speaks who has been told something, has accepted it, but has not understood it. "It is the same god—but before we did not know about him properly."

"And now you do?"

"Na-Groth tells us about him."

"And who is this Na-Groth?"

Isar could feel the thrill of cold fear that went through the people at the tone of his voice.

"He is Groth's spokesman. Groth speaks through him.

Isar was silent. It was plain that no amount of sceptical mockery from him would counteract the fear with which these people regarded Na-Groth and his god.

"And what of the Spirits?" he said at last. "Do they not speak to your hearts in the Silent times and tell you of your God and His ways?"

"Na-Groth says we must not go into the Silence. He says that only he knows the ways of Groth. He says the Spirits do not exist. He says that nothing speaks to us in the Silence but our own desires and fears."

Isar's heart was beating fast. He began to see what had happened here and how far it had gone.

He too began to feel the fear and the despair.

Fear and despair! Were these the inward marks of the new religion, as wound and scar were the outward?

Was it possible his own people had misunderstood the nature of God?

He thought back to the quiet field-strips and villages he had left behind so recently, which now seemed locked in some bygone age, with his childhood. He thought of the confidence he used to feel that all the great and distant stars above his head and the familiar grains of sand beneath his feet were contributing with all the Realms of Being, visible and invisible, to a pattern of great magnificence, each in harmony with each, each dependent on the other.

His silence worried the villagers. They began to move about uneasily. A look-out was posted at the doorway, and there was murmuring amongst them. Was the traveller a spy of Na-Groth after all? Had he falsely led them on to trap them?

Isar felt helpless.

Their anxiety preyed on his spirit. He felt it con-

suming him, and he had to work hard to regain his
own inner strength.

"No," he said at last, "I am no spy. I am a traveller
and I am weary. Does this village not sleep when night
comes to it?"

Keel took his arm, remembering suddenly with joy,
the old ways of hospitality.

"We sleep indeed, though dreams are not welcome
to us these nights. But first we eat. Woman, what are
you about that you have not prepared the evening
meal?"

Isar felt the injustice of Keel's remark for the
woman, but she did not seem to mind.

Soon the bustle of preparing the evening meal did
away with all the tension.

By the time they came to roll up in their rugs there
was peace in the house and there were some who did
not remember Na-Groth in their sleep.

Isar slept long and soundly, weary beyond any weariness he had ever felt before.

The priests of the Temple of the Sun were able to turn
Isar's journey to meet the wood-carver Janak to their
advantage.

Through Kyra's reading of the messenger's last
thoughts, they were now well aware of the situation in
Klad, and the Inner Council decided that Isar was not
to be brought home to safety, but was to be sent farther into Klad to seek out Na-Groth and destroy him.

The priesthood had great powers, but they were still

limited to human frames and needed human channels for their work.

The priests of Klad had been killed, and though they might still be capable of helping in certain subtle ways within the deepest levels of consciousness, they too could only work through someone still physically upon the earth.

Isar, although not a priest or a novitiate, was sensitive to more levels of reality than most men. He could be of great help to them.

The Lady Kyra and the Lord Khu-ren worked far into the night among the Tall Stones of the Temple to contact his spirit, to strengthen and instruct it in the task it had before it.

They called on the Spirit Realms and were given Isar's secret name, the one he had through all time and which was known only in the Spirit Realms. There were times of crisis when it was possible for humans as highly evolved as the Lords of the Sun to call on the Spirits for this knowledge and be given it to hold in trust until the crisis had passed.

These secret names were not given lightly, for the knowledge of them carried great power and humans were not on the whole to be trusted with such authority.

Kyra and Khu-ren knew that when they had reached Isar his secret name would fall so deep into the hidden places of their minds that they would never again remember it with their surface consciousness. Nor would they forget it, for nothing that is experienced is ever totally forgotten.

It would be hidden until they too entered the Spirit Realms and were capable of remembering it without danger to Isar.

Now, murmuring his names, his given name and his secret name, they passed from Stone to Stone of the Inner Sanctum, touching the Sacred Rocks with their foreheads, with each touching, the humming and vibrating of the rocks that was imperceptible to ordinary people, growing in their consciousness until it seemed to them the Universe was filled with noise and energy through which the two names of Isar reverberated like giant drums.

In their home beside the Temple their daughter Deva lay staring into the dark, her eyes stubbornly open against sleep, daring the darkness and the evil god called Groth to touch her lord Isar. Her thoughts were fierce and protective but they were only the selfish thoughts of a young girl in love, and went no further than the chamber in which she lay.

Groth and Na-Groth were not aware of them.

Nor was Isar, lost to consciousness, deep in Kyra's strangely refreshing sleep.

Nor were the villagers of Klad tossing uneasily at his side, worrying about the morning and what it would bring.

Towards dawn Deva's body refused to obey any longer the commands of her body to vigilance. She fell asleep like a grey feather from a bird and lay snuggled in her fur rugs, a child again.

She had not been asleep long when she began to notice that she was in a place she had often visited before in dreams, particularly when she was troubled. It was a place she recognized when she was asleep, but not when she was awake. If she had been there at all, ever, during her waking time, it must have been in a former life.

The place was a garden. Flowers grew there that did not grow near her waking home. The earth was sandy and reddish and a ring of small fountains, catching the intense sunlight and reflecting it like silver, arose from a circular pool curbed with slabs of pure white stone.

Sometimes she stood on the stone pavement gazing down into the white slabs, noticing that they were of a crystalline structure so fine that she could look into them and see the crystals in the depths as easily as those on the surface.

At other times she looked towards the pool and through the veil of spinning, moving drops of silver liquid she could see purple water flowers growing, glowing with such intensity of light that it seemed they were alight themselves and were not reflecting the sun.

During one "dream" she looked up and thought she saw a roof of transparent rock crystal held up by a ring of tall, slender white columns. The sunlight was concentrated through the rock crystal canopy in such a way that a beam of brilliance that hurt the eyes shone down upon the water flowers so that they seemed to dissolve in light and she could only "feel" that they were there, "remember" that they were there, but she could not see them.

At such times she felt great reverence and awe as though she were in the presence of something beyond our Reality.

But there were times when, although the place was beautiful, it seemed ordinary, and she found herself playing among the trees and shrubs with a small, sleek black cat.

She was a child. This was her garden and her cat.

Once, enclosed in green shrubs, unseen, she watched two men walk in the garden. One was tall and vigorous, speaking with his hands to emphasize his words, the other a calmer, older man dressed with careful elegance.

She knew the older man was the king and the younger man was her father. She was proud of him. He was a great philosopher and architect, at this very moment engaged in supervising the construction of a remakable building . . . a building that pierced the sky with one sharp golden point, drawing power from the mysterious Spirit Realms and dispersing it down the sloping triangular sides of stone into the earth, north, south, east and west.

This night when Deva, who lived now in the body in another time and another place, visited the ancient garden in her sleep, she carried with her the faint remembrance of Isar and his dangers. The beauty of the fountains and the water flowers could not hold her. She was impatient with her playmate cat and walked distractedly among the green bowers, searching for her father.

The parents of her present body would not bring Isar out of danger, but expected him alone to challenge the might of Na-Groth and his god.

She would ask nothing of them again.

Something in her longed for former times and homed upon an ancient love.

But she was too anxious, her mind too active and demanding. Instead of allowing the "dream" to take her into the garden and make its own shape, she tried to force the image of her former father to appear, and he eluded her.

Dismayed, she saw the lovely place dissolve around her and found herself awake with only longing in her heart and no comfort to sustain her through another day of anxiety.

The Chase

Isar was awakened by a girl shaking his shoulder. He remembered her among the group of villagers who had surrounded him in the house the evening before, but she had kept silent while the others had been questioning him. She was a little older than Deva, pale and thin, her bones almost protruding through her skin, her eyes large and expressive.

Struggling with the unnaturally deep sleep that had fallen upon him and was now so rudely being dispelled, Isar opened his mouth and tried to muster his thick and sluggish tongue to ask what the matter was. He felt as though part of him was awake and the rest was struggling behind, trying to catch up.

Seeing his lips move, her thin fingers went to her mouth and she shook her head. He stared stupidly at her. She pointed to the figures lying around him still locked in sleep and again indicated that he should make no sound. First light was creeping through the doorway and he could see the shapes of the other occupants of the house like humps and hillocks in the half dark.

She tugged at his arm, determined that he should wake and follow her.

His eyes began to close again. He was still weary and confused.

She pulled his rugs from him and roughly poked and tugged at him to force him awake. Through the haze of his sleepiness he caught an impression of fear and urgency in her movements. He began to realize that he might be in danger and that she was trying to warn him.

Suddenly he was fully alert.

So urgent was her insistence that he had barely time to gather his belongings together before she had him stooping and crouching and creeping to the door of the house. She went ahead of him and held him back with her hand while she made sure all was clear outside.

He followed her unquestioningly when she gestured him on.

It was early indeed and the village, half hidden in mist, its inhabitants still lost in sleep, seemed ghostly and unreal.

The air was chill and the grass wet from the night's rain.

He held her hand and allowed himself to be led away from the village, first to a clump of trees and then, stumbling and slithering a bit, up a muddy hill.

Every time he tried to open his mouth to ask a question she put her finger on his lips and he was silent.

When they reached the top she pulled him down beside her amongst the long wet grass and pointed to a winding path, barely visible, to the south west of the village.

At first he saw nothing but the track threading brown amongst the grass and bracken, but soon he caught a sound followed almost immediately by the sight of a group of men emerging from the mist and bearing down upon the houses.

As they drew nearer Isar noticed that they were led by one of the villagers, one who had not joined the others in sleep but had crept from the house when the questioning was at its height. The men behind him were larger than he, dressed in dark leather, carrying staves and armed with axes and swords. They stepped in time with each other in a way that made Isar shudder. It was as though by giving up their individuality of movement, they gave up their humanity.

He looked at the girl's tense face and knew that she had saved his life.

"Thank you," he whispered, "may the Spirit Realms keep you as safe as you have kept me."

She shook her head slightly and there were lines of anxiety still upon her pale face. She pointed away from the village.

He followed her gaze. Was there further danger there?

She tugged his arm and he knew he must follow her yet again. The men were out of sight now, but it was not safe to stay so near the village. If the informer had convinced them that there was a traveller from the east present without the Mark of Groth upon his forehead, they would certainly scour the countryside until they found him.

"Where can we go?" he whispered to the girl.

Again she put her finger on her lips. Again he fell silent and followed her.

They had travelled a long way and the grass was already dry in the morning sunlight before she allowed him to rest.

Sitting with his back against a mossy rock he turned to her and said: "I owe my life to you, but I do not know your name."

A sad shadow flitted across her face and she turned away from him, staring out across the wild and rocky moor that stretched to the south of them.

Thinking that she had not understood, he repeated the question more slowly, emphasizing every word, as he would for a person who did not speak his language.

"Your name?"

She was silent still.

He took her arm and turned her to face himself, and then he put his hand on his own chest.

"My name," he said distinctly, "is Isar."

And then he pointed to her and his expression was questioning.

"Your name?"

She shook her head sadly.

He looked at her, unsure what to do next.

She looked at him long and thoughtfully and then

half opened her mouth as though she were about to say something, but shut it again before she did.

His eyes on her were so intense and curious, so gentle and so warm with friendliness she seemed to take heart to try again. But this time she opened her mouth wide and pointed to the inside of it.

Puzzled, he leaned forward and looked into her mouth.

And then he understood.

"O no!" he whispered.

Na-Groth had not only put the mark of slavery upon her forehead, he had cut out her tongue as well!

He drew back in momentary revulsion at what he had seen and then he realized that her eyes were still upon him and she had noticed his reaction and had been hurt by it.

Tears were welling up in her eyes.

Filled with regret for the tactlessness of his expression and bitterness at the cruelty of Na-Groth, he took her hands, pulled her tenderly towards him and kissed the scar on her forehead.

She smiled for the first time since he had seen her and with that smile her thin, gaunt face became beautiful and full of light.

"But you can hear and understand?" he asked.

She nodded vigorously.

He thought about the situation.

He did not know how she had known that his presence had been betrayed, but it would be clear to Na-Groth's men that she had helped him to escape.

There could be no going back to her home village.

She would have to come with him.

But where was he going?

He looked at the open moor to the south, the hills behind him and to the east. The east was where he longed to be, but between him and his home lay unknown country filled with alert and hostile men.

He looked at the girl and his brow was creased with worry.

She was sitting with her knees drawn up and her chin resting upon them, staring unseeingly into the distance. The light had gone out of her face. She was exiled from her home and friends, companion of a fugitive.

Isar shut his eyes tightly and then opened them wide, hoping to find that the whole thing was nothing more than a bad dream.

But it was not a dream.

"We cannot sit here forever," he said at last, decisively. "You have saved my life and taken me from danger and it is now my turn to do this for you. It will not be easy, but we must return to my people and fetch help."

To his surprise the girl shook her head.

"What do you mean? You will not come with me?"

She shook her head.

"You *will* come with me?"

She nodded affirmatively.

"What then? Why did you shake your head?"

She pointed to the west and nodded, pointed to the east and shook her head.

He frowned. Was she saying that they must go deeper into Klad?

She pointed yet again, vigorously, to the western hills.

"But why?" he demanded, frustrated that she could not answer.

She shrugged helplessly, but pointed yet again and her face showed her determination.

"No," he said, "you are wrong in this. There is nothing we can do against Na-Groth by ourselves. No, do not nod your head at me! Believe me, there is *nothing* we can do. We *must* go east and bring help from the Great Temple."

He could see she was going to be stubborn about this, but he decided it was up to him to make the decisions. He pulled her up by her arm and turned her towards the east.

In order to make her come with him he had to hold her roughly and drag her along. She tried many times to break away and turn them back and her determination began to make him doubt that he was doing the right thing.

What if she had some good reason for going west?

But if she had she could not tell him, and he chose to believe that it was her fear of the unknown that kept her tied to her own country in spite of everything.

After a while she tired of fighting him and walked beside him without being held, but her face was sulky and her eyes were downcast.

They made good progress although sometimes they had to weave backwards and forwards across the country to avoid groups of Na-Groth's warriors and villagers they could not trust.

The sun had just passed its zenith when she held him back and began to look around her nervously like a young doe sensing danger.

At first he could hear nothing, but he remained still, respecting her superior sensitivity to danger.

And then, borne on a breeze, he heard distinctly what she had already heard, the distant bark and howl of dogs on the hunt.

He had heard packs of wild dogs in the forests and had feared them and pitied their hapless prey, but there was something mingled with the sound this time that made his body suddenly cold.

The throats of men were uttering sounds as savage as the dogs. Together they were hunting and together they were coming nearer.

The girl and Isar looked at each other and knew, without any doubt, that they were the prey.

They looked around desperately.

Where was there to run?

Where to hide?

It was the girl who made the decision.

She seized Isar's hand and they ran and slid and stumbled back down the hill they had just climbed so laboriously in the heat of the day, she turned him into the wood at the foot of the hill, through it and out the other side. She was making towards a gleam of water she had noticed earlier.

His lungs were aching with the effort, his blood hammering in his ears, but, louder than the hammering was the ghastly howl and jabber of the hunters as they came nearer.

The girl gave his hand a sudden tug and before he knew what was happening he was plunging off a low cliff into a lake. The shock of the cold water banged all his breath from him and, gasping and choking, he allowed himself to be pulled by the girl, who so much smaller and frailer than he, could swim with the strength and precision of a fish. She guided him under an overhang of rock and they hid close to the slimy, muddy bed of the lake edge, their heads obscured in water reeds and shadowed by the overhanging cliff.

They could still hear the dogs, but they could not see them.

Isar struggled to regain his breath. Mud and water weed plastered his head and the girl herself looked uncommonly like a rat, her face was so pinched and thin, her hair so closely bedraggled about her face. At another time he would have laughed, but now it was all he could do to keep hidden and prevent himself coughing.

The dogs were confused by the lake and led their human counterparts in several directions. Isar could hear the angry shouting of the men and thought perhaps they would be safe at last, but then he noticed that they had found a way down to the water's edge and were beating the reeds to find them. Startled water birds sprang up screeching and flew off in every direction. The air was noisy with shouting, barking, howling, yelping, screeching and the beat of stick on reed and wing on wing.

The girl pulled him under the water and started to swim towards the centre of the lake. He followed, though swimming did not come easily to him. His movements were clumsy compared to hers, but he managed somehow, his lungs almost bursting with the effort of holding his breath under water.

They had to surface.

There was no way to hold their breath longer.

In fear and dread they broke cover, took deep gulps of air and plunged again.

So quickly had they dived they had no time to ascertain whether they had been noticed by the hunters.

They had to swim on, not knowing if their pursuers would be waiting for them when they reached the shore or not.

Everything had happened so quickly Isar had not had time to grasp the full reality of the situation.

Now, in the murk of the cold and clouded water, his aching lungs told him that death could be very near.

A wave of longing to live flowed through him like pain.

Why had he let the days pass by so casually?

Why had he not shot each moment like a golden arrow, using to the full the bow of life he had been given so freely as a gift?

He knew death was not final, but only the entrance to other Realms of Being . . . but . . . he enjoyed being Isar. He did not want to change . . . not yet . . .

"O Lord of Spirit, Lord of Sun, Lord of the Circle out of which there is no passing . . . give me longer as Isar . . . longer to love those that I love . . . longer that I may bring help to the people under the shadow of Groth!"

His head broke the surface of the water . . . the sun burst with light into his eyes and he could see nothing but brightness and gold.

Blinking and dazed, he could feel the young stranger's hand in his and his clothes dragging on him and the mud of the lake bed sucking at his feet as he stumbled and struggled out on to the pebbles of the shore.

The voices of his enemies were in the distance.

He looked back and saw them still beating the reeds on the other side. Unquestioningly he followed the girl into the woods that bordered the lake and that mercifully hid them from their pursuers.

But she would not let him rest until the sun was setting, and then they fell upon the hill side, aching in every limb, caked with dried mud, scratched and torn by briars, but alive, and safe at last from the hounds who had lost their scent.

Isar, lying on the ground, staring up at the strange luminous blue of the sky just before night fall, saw a lark soar high above them and heard its sweet call as it turned to find its nest.

"I shall call you Lark," he said. "You remind me of a lark."

The girl looked at him, puzzled. A lark is noted for its song, and she had no voice.

He smiled and understood her thought.

"You are small and light and swift. You ride high and see further than most of us. You do not sing with words, but I hear the sweetness of your voice in my head," he said, and he closed his eyes sleepily. "Besides," and his thoughts seemed to continue in his dreams, "the lark is a sacred bird and leads men to the safety of the Spirit Realms."

The Sacrilege

Slowly the Spear-lord's wife, Isar's mother, Fern, walked amongst the green profusion of her garden. The sunset had been magnificent, but for once she had not bowed her head to it, nor murmured the customary words of evening prayer.

This coming darkness brought one more night of danger to her much loved son and the prayer she must say must not be one of custom, but of power and sincerity.

As she walked she gently touched the darkening branches of her Rowan tree, called with her heart that all that lived and grew, rooted in the earth and drawing strength from sun and air, would hear her and convey wariness to Isar, strength of purpose, sharpness of senses.

She sank upon her knees and lowered her forehead to the earth.

She listened to the minute earth sounds of growing roots, of burrowing earth worms, the slow suck and slither of slug and snail. Deep in the earth she felt the process of decay and renewal as once dead matter was slowly changed into a new cycle of life. Below that she could detect the restless shift and grind as strata of rock deep buried sought new levels and readjusted to old. Nothing stayed the same.

She could not hold Isar immobile, to be broken by the slow chisel of time. She did not ask that.

But tears nevertheless fell on the soft grass for what could never be.

"What are you doing?" a deep voice spoke above her, and she looked up the full length of Karne, her husband, who seemed, from this angle, to be a giant.

He took her in his arms and lifted her up. He saw the tears on her cheeks. Gently he wiped away the small shreds of grass and stick that adhered to her soft skin.

"I was praying," she whispered with a catch in her voice as she tried to stop herself weeping.

He held her close.

He kissed her deeply on the lips.

At first she surrendered to the kiss and felt comforted by its intensity. But a cold feeling began to come over her and she pulled herself sharply back.

Had she imagined there was the taste of parting in the kiss?

She looked at him.

He was in his travelling cloak, a broad leather belt fastening his sword to his side, leather on his arms for protection, and, over his shoulder, the fighting bow he had not used since Wardyke's war.

He put his fingers to her lips.

"I know, I know," he said softly. "But it has to be. You must stay at home and pray, but I must go and seek him. I will bring him back to you. I swear it!"

"How can you swear it?" she said fiercely, weeping, her voice harsh. "Do you know all that the Spirits know? Are you God Himself that you can order a man's destiny?"

"Destiny comes from men's thoughts and men's actions working within the limited Circle of our Existence. The Lord who wears the whole of our universe as though it were one bead upon a necklace will not deny my right to use my body and my mind while I have them, in the way that seems right to me."

Fern wanted Isar safely back more than anything in the world and she trusted Karne greately, but, what if Karne were lost to her as well as Isar . . . how would she live?

"You must not think those thoughts," chided Karne, seeing her expression. "I will take care. There are other men coming, but I cannot wait until they are all assembled and ready." Karne had never been noted for his patience! "I will go ahead and when they arrive I will know the situation exactly and what the plan must be."

"Does Kyra know that you are going?"

Fern dried her eyes, knowing that it was useless to continue fighting the inevitable.

"No. You will tell her, my love, when I am safely gone."

"But . . ."

"I am going. The Temple is slow to resort to arms and busy with the devious ways of mind and spirit. In case they do not work, I and other armed men will be ready."

"It is a long way to Klad," she said forlornly, "the methods of the Temple may be the only ones that will be effective and in time."

"No one wil be more pleased than I if their methods work. I go only in case they do not."

"And because you cannot sit around and do nothing no matter how many priests command it!" A flicker of amusement passed through Fern's eyes.

He smiled broadly and touched her under the chin, looking down into the golden brown depths of her eyes with amused tenderness.

"I love you," he said and then, suddenly solemn, "I *will* take care."

She watched him go, the green curtain of creeper that hung from tree to tree making a kind of archway, hiding him from her sight almost immediately.

The night would be soon upon him. A patient man would have waited until dawn. But Fern knew that every man must do things in his own way, at his own pace.

His way was not her way, nor the way of the Temple, but that did not mean it was wrong.

The same night that saw the beginning of Karne's journey, and Isar sleeping upon the hillside in Klad worn out by the pursuit of the hunting dogs, found Deva in sleep far away in time and place, walking in the garden of her former life.

After the experience of the night before she had not tried to come to the garden, but had deliberately tried to think of other things at the time of going to bed.

She lay flat on her back in her rugs and thought about Isar, not the danger he was now in, but the happy times they had had together.

She remembered how she used to sit beside him while he carved figures in wood, sometimes for her and sometimes for other people. Grown-up people made a great fuss over his work and took it for their homes.

She had been with him a few summers ago when he had been carving the Sacred Symbols into the wood of the great columns that lined the entrance to the Temple from the ceremonial avenue.

There had always been wooden columns marking the entrance, but it was Kyra who suggested to the Inner Council that Isar should mark them with the Sacred Signs.

"I have seen those marks on houses," Deva said.

"You have seen them everywhere."

"And on stone . . ." Deva continued thoughtfully.

"Everywhere!" he said vaguely, pausing briefly in his work to wave his hand, his gesture taking in the Circle of the great Temple, the low hills studded with burial mounds surrounding it, the sky surrounding the hills.

She looked around, puzzled.

"You mean everything seems to go in circles, and the signs are circles within circles?"

He nodded abstractedly, concentrating on pressing his blade into the hard, dark wood at just the right angle, to draw it with all his strength against the grain.

"Is it because our eyes are round that we see round?" she demanded.

He did not answer.

"Or does everything go round anyway, quite apart from how we see it?"

He was still silent, concentrating on his work.

She stood beside him, a small figure determined not to be ignored, silent for a few moments, but soon with another question.

"Why do you put that sort of path from the inside to the outside?"

"Or from the outside to the inside," he said enigmatically.

She was beginning to get very irritated with him.

"I do not think very much of our secret symbols," she said boldly, lifting her chin, her black eyes flashing at him.

This gave him pause and he looked at her shocked.

Pleased with the effect of her last words she decided to give him something else to think about.

"I have seen much more interesting symbols carved on stone columns in a garden I go to sometimes."

He was silent for a few moments.

He stood up and looked straight into her eyes.

He knew Deva was mischievous and could not always be relied on to tell the truth, especially when she was trying to attract attention to herself.

"What sort of symbols?"

"Birds and animals and . . . men looking sideways . . . sometimes men with animal heads . . . all sorts of different things!"

"Where is this garden?"

"It is a secret."

"I thought as much," he said. "You are making it up."

"I am *not*," she said hotly.

But she had lost his attention and he went back to his carving, an irritating expression of disbelief on his face.

She was furious and stood silent and fuming for what seemed a long while, and then she took one of his best knives and while he was not looking carved some of the tiny figures she had seen in her "dream" garden on a sliver of flat chalk stone she found beside her on the ground.

They both worked silently, completely absorbed in what they were doing. It was the arrival of the Lord Khu-ren, her father, that shattered their concentration.

Deva would never forget the next few moments. In them she learnt how painful it was for her when Isar was angry with her, and also that her "dream" garden might very well have a reality she had not before been sure about.

Khu-ren found the two young people apparently peacefully and harmoniously at work together, and he greeted them lovingly.

Isar looked up and saw Deva using his best wood-carving knife on stone, and with an unaccustomed shout of rage seized it, cutting her finger accidentally as he did so.

She screamed as blood spurted out.

The peaceful scene was instantly transformed to one of chaos. Isar was shouting, partly with anger about his knife and partly with horror at what he had done.

Deva had the attention she wanted and used every trick to keep it. The cut was not really very painful but she made a great fuss and was carried off by her father to have it bound with healing leaves and cobweb.

Isar trailed behind, distraught and anxious, convinced he had maimed her for life.

When Khu-ren straightened out her clenched hand to bind the finger, the piece of carved chalk stone, now stained with blood, fell on to his knee. He put it aside while he was working on her hand, but when the bleeding was staunched and the two youngsters started grumbling at each other again for what had happened, he picked up the chalk stone in order to distract their attention from their grievances.

"What is this?" he asked, holding it out and looking at it carefully, expecting to see that Deva had been copying the Sacred Symbols Isar was carving on the wooden column.

Instead he saw, carved crudely but unmistakably, the symbols of his own land, the land of the desert and the Great River, that he had left so deliberately behind when he was a young man.

His face grew grave and he stared at the carved stone long and intensely.

Deva and Isar became silent.

They could see his change of mood and were at a loss to understand it.

He repeated his question, but his voice was now stern and serious.

Deva was a little frightened. Her father could be very formidable at times.

Seeing that she could not answer, Isar spoke quickly for her, as he had often done before when her mischief had led her into trouble.

"It is nothing," he said.

"Nothing?" Khu-ren said pointedly, holding out the piece of stone for Isar to see.

Isar saw some extremely clumsy scratchings, one of which resembled a bird with very long legs, and one that could have been a man but he seemed deformed. His body was facing forwards, but his feet and head were facing sideways.

He looked puzzled. Why should this make Khu-ren so grave?

"Where have you seen these things?" the High Priest demanded of the little girl.

Nervously she shook her head.

"Nowhere," she whispered drily.

He looked at her with the same black eyes as her own, long and penetratingly. Then he looked at Isar.

"She . . . she said she saw them in a secret garden. But I think she was just making up stories as usual," Isar said.

Deva flushed with the injustice of this remark, but was not sure enough of herself to contradict it. She seemed to be in some kind of trouble because of the scratchings, but she did not know why. She decided to stay quiet until she was certain of her position.

"They . . . they are very good," Isar ventured now, feeling sorry for her. "Do you not think so, my lord?"

"No," said Khu-ren, "I do not think so. And I do not like lies either."

Isar put his arm around Deva and she snuggled up to him.

"My lord!" He lifted his chin to speak defiantly, but before he could say more Khu-ren held up his hand to silence him.

Isar was silent, not because of the authority of the High Priest's gesture, for he would have dared anyone to protect Deva, but because he could see the man's mood had changed again.

"Never mind," Khu-ren said. "We may be making too much of this. They are just the idle scratchings of a little girl after all. I am sorry I frightened you," he said to Deva and kissed the top of her head. "Run along now!" He waved them away and went off himself, but Deva noticed with rage that he took her piece of stone with him.

"Idle scratchings!" she said bitterly. "I will have you know that they are copies of symbols I have seen in the most beautiful garden in the world. They are from columns that hold up a roof to make a shady walk around the garden because the sun is very hot there. Much hotter than here!" she said fiercely to Isar.

"Your fair skin would be burnt to ashes there. But mine would be all right!" she added proudly.

Something stirred in Isar's memory, something from his childhood. He had known once, but the knowledge was as vague as dream knowledge, that he and Deva had lived and loved before in ancient times and the garden she described seemed fleetingly familiar to him too. But the image was too unclear. He could not be sure.

"You must tell me more about your garden," he said gently to her, stroking her black silky hair soothingly.

"You said I was making up stories!" she said sulkily.

"I was wrong," he said humbly. "It is very easy to be wrong about things."

They found a bank to sit upon and she told him about her "dream" visits and what she had seen there.

He listened intently but could not say truthfully he believed she was really visiting an ancient garden (in memory), or whether she was dreaming about an imaginary garden.

But then he thought about the scratchings on the stone and how disturbed Khu-ren had been.

It was strange.

Midsummer had come and gone four times since then and now he lay upon an alien hillside with danger all around him, a girl who could not speak beside him, and Deva wrapped in her rugs in the High Priest's house, and yet walking in a garden half a world away in a time long since passed.

This time Deva had drifted into the garden while she was thinking of Isar and the occasion when he had cut her finger. Surprised, she still felt pain in the same finger in her dream, and looked down at her hand. A small snake was slithering away across the hot paving stones and she knew she had been bitten.

She screamed.

Someone came running.

It was a boy, slightly older than herself. Someone she had never seen before. Someone lithe and muscular and dark, someone who excited her so much that she stood still, holding her finger tightly to stop the poisoned blood flowing, but making no sound.

Within moments he had a dagger in his hand and was cutting her finger. He seemed so sure of himself she made no murmur though she expected the pain to be extreme. Having cut, he sucked and spat the mixture of blood and venom on to the smooth white crystal of the paving stones. She stared at it with horror, dazed by the suddenness of it all.

He was still sucking and spitting when the king's guards came running and seized him, beat him and dragged him away.

"No! No!" she screamed, but they did not listen to her. She tried to run after them, to explain, but she began to feel as though she were falling and everything was growing dark around her.

She must have fainted.

Time in that ancient land must have passed, because when she became conscious again she was lying in a strange room on a bed of black wood with four gold panther heads at each corner.

Men were bending over her.

One was her father.

She lifted her arms to him at once and struggled to tell him of the boy who had saved her life, and must himself be saved.

He soothed her with his large and finely shaped hands, he gazed at her with loving concern, but he did not understand a word that she was saying.

Desperately she sought the right words.

The words that came made sense to her, but not to the men who surrounded her.

She looked around in despair.

She was caught between two life times.

She was at once the girl of the garden, the daughter of the architect, who had been bitten by a snake and rescued by a boy who should not have been in the king's garden, and yet she was speaking in the language of Deva who lived now in another life and in another time.

Weeping with frustration she found herself awake in Deva's own time, Kyra at her side questioning her gently about her bad dream.

"It was not a dream," she sobbed. "It was not a dream!"

"The garden again?" Kyra asked softly.

Deva did not answer, but her mother knew by her face that it was so.

"Tell me," she commanded softly.

Deva was wide awake and sitting up fiercely.

"I will tell you *nothing*, lady, until you bring Isar home."

Kyra shook her head sadly.

"You do not help Isar this way, daughter," she said. "Nor yourself."

"*You* do not help him lady! You do not help him!" she cried bitterly.

"There is no help in former times. '*Now*' is the material we have to work with. *Now* we try everything in our power to help him and ourselves."

"Have you spoken with him? Have you found him?"

Deva clasped her mother's hands, for the moment forgetting that she had sworn to ask her nothing until she brought Isar home.

Kyra's face was grave.

"We think we gave him deep and restful sleep . . ."

"Is that all!" Deva cried in anguish.

"A rested and refreshed mind and body could make the difference between life and death in such a situation of danger."

"But have you not *spoken* with him?"

"I was on my way to the Temple when I heard you cry out," Kyra said.

"O no!" Deva was in despair again.

Her mother rose.

"Gently, my love," she said tenderly. "Tonight the moon is full, the stars are right, and the powers of the Stones will be at their greatest. Tonight we will reach him. Do not fear."

But Deva did fear.

Their communication with him could only mean greater danger for him. They were not going to call him home. They were going to "use" him to do their work in Klad.

She lay in the dark tossing and turning, sleep impossible, reasonable trust and patience far from her. The darkness seemed to press upon her like a suffocating incubus mocking her helplessness, whispering to her of Isar's danger.

She had failed him once long ago when he had been flogged and imprisoned for trespassing in the king's garden, and she was failing him again.

Where Kyra had moved the door skins to allow her exit, a wedge of blue-grey remained, drawing Deva's eye.

There was a way out of the darkness if only she had the nerve to take it.

The dark hole of her chamber had a doorway. Outside the doorway the full moon was climbing steadily above the Temple, the Sacred place of Tall Stones, the Inner Sanctum which was forbidden to non-initiates.

She sat up, cold and rigid with fear at the daring idea that had come to her.

She rose instantly, her decision made.

She took light from the torch that burnt all night beside the entrance to their house and lit several little chalk-stone oil lamps.

She searched her mother's chamber for the robes she had worn when the messenger from Klad had arrived.

With trembling hands she transformed herself into

the semblance of a priest and set upon her head the diadem of jet Kyra had worn at her inauguration.

Time was passing and she must not be late.

Where was the long blue cloak that would complete the image?

Her mind was racing.

There was a kind of justice in the fact that to save his life she had to trespass in a forbidden place just as he had done at their first meeting in that other life so long ago.

There was no doubt that she would be punished too.

But nothing mattered to her except his safe return.

She found the cloak at last and drew it about herself.

The moon was high enough for her to need no torch and she flitted unseen from shadow to shadow until she neared the Temple entrance. Then she walked boldly forward as though she had the right to pass into the Sacred Circle.

The young priest who had been set at the entrance to warn away anyone not part of the night's work half raised a hand to stop her, but let it fall again as she swept elegantly past him.

Once within the Circle she came to rest in the shadow of one of the Giant Stones that rimmed the outer bank. From there she could see without being seen the ceremony taking place in the Northern Inner Sanctum.

She wanted to be sure she knew the position of everyone before she moved.

Up to now she had been so intent upon her purpose

she had had no warning pangs to give her pause, but now the majesty of the scene before her filled her with the beginnings of doubt and fear.

The Great Temple was always an impressive sight and held within its high sloping banks and its circle of giant Sacred Stones a kind of powerful energy that ordinary people found almost too strong to bear. Deva could feel it now. The whole scene seemed charged with significance and power. The shadows of the rocks were blacker than ordinary shadows and lay at the feet of their masters like deep holes leading into the earth. The Stones themselves gleamed eerily in the moonlight and the figures of the priests moving around the Sanctum seemed at once very small next to the Tall Stones and yet very large compared to their normal selves. The darkness of their cloaked bodies was like the darkness of the shadows, as though she was looking not *at* them, but through them into . . . unimaginable depths of Being . . . pure consciousness, without form . . .

Deva tried to stop herself trembling by reminding herself that she saw these men and women every day and they were not much different from herself.

But even as she told herself this the power of the Temple began to work on her and she began to see the contrast between her own selfish, short-term desire to rescue her love, and their greater and more comprehensive one, to rescue a whole people.

She put her hands to her ears as though the words were reaching her from outside.

"I *will not* listen," she hissed. "He *must* be brought back. There *will be* another way to save our land!"

Afraid to wait a moment longer she made her move and slid across the grass like the shadow of a snake, until she was just outside the inner ring of Stones where the priests were working.

The priests stood just outside the Circle, each marking a Stone, each with his eyes closed, deep in concentration.

At the very centre the two Lords of the Sun moved from Stone to Stone of the Sacred Inner Three, murmuring softly and touching their foreheads reverently to the ancient channels of power between Earth and Sky, Body and Spirit.

Deva leapt into the Circle and stood as though frozen in Time, hearing as loud as thunder what had been incomprehensible murmuring to her a moment before, the given name of Isar and following it the Secret Name she had no right to hear.

With the hearing of it the Moon that rode in the white light above them seemed to explode and lightning burst from it, touching the tip of every Stone in the Great Circle.

Horrified, Deva saw herself in a cage of white fire, the faces of the priests huge around her, their eyes like black sockets in their heads.

"Isar!" she screamed and then, with all the passion in her body, the Dread Name she was never meant to know.

With the speaking of it pain when through her like a sword and she fell into darkness like a pebble into a bottomless pit.

"Deva!" screamed Kyra, priest no more, but mother rushing to her child.

"Deva!" gasped Khu-ren.

The priests outside the ring opened their eyes and stared astonished at the scene before them.

They had heard and seen nothing, but had felt the sudden shattering of the vibrations that had held them locked into trance.

Now they saw the two Lords of the Sun stooping over a third figure, lifting it to the moonlight. For a moment they fancied it was Isar returned magically in some way by the power of the incantation, but as the pale light fell on the face of the limp figure they saw it was the beautiful girl child of the High Priest and the Lady Kyra, Deva, who charmed and plagued them as they went about their business in the Temple community.

They drew closer, but did not dare to cross the invisible line that divided the Inner Circle from the Outer.

In Klad Isar jerked awake, his name exploding in his head.

He sat up and looked around him, bewildered, his heart pounding. He half expected to find himself at the centre of a thunder storm, but everything was strangely calm. The moon was full and brilliant, throwing the landscape into relief, picking out with light the beaded threads of streams and flat surfaces, darkening the shadows of cliffs and trees and rocks.

Awake he was not sure that it had been his name that he had heard. Asleep it had seemed to belong to him and he had responded, but now he knew it was not Isar. He struggled to remember it more clearly but already it was slipping away from him like water draining into sand.

He looked at his companion. She was curled up, her knees drawn up to her chin, sleeping soundly.

Should he wake her and suggest that they travel on? He was refreshed and restless now, anxious to move, troubled by the strangeness of his experience.

It was light enough to find their way and probably safer than by daylight.

He began to long for home with a desperation that was almost an ache . . . Home where there was quiet and peace, long hours to sit carving or dreaming, helping his mother tend the growing things of the garden, carrying the water from the spring for her. She always wanted water from the spring rather than from the stream, which was nearer.

"It comes from deep in the rock. It is fresh and clear and full of earth energy. Drink. You will see what I mean."

Thinking of that water now gave him a thirst.

He touched Lark's shoulder and she sprang up, instantly on the defensive, fear and the moonlight making her eyes gleam unnaturally in the dark.

He was sorry that he had woken her and tried to tell her so. He tried to explain the name he had heard in his head.

"I am certain I was being called home."

He could not see the expression on her face.

"We will move on now. It will be safer at night. Easier to hide from Na-Groth's men."

She nodded and gathered herself together turning towards the west.

"No!" he said. "I am going home. I have been called home. They know there is nothing I can do against Na-Groth."

She did not turn, but continued to gaze in the direction she wished to go.

"What do you want me to do?" he burst out angrily. "What could I possibly *hope* to do!"

He hated her silence. How he longed for talkative little Deva!

The girl's quiet was confronting him with a decision he did not want to make.

"Well, I cannot help it," he said at last, "if you want to go and throw yourself at Na-Groth's feet I cannot stop you. But *I* am going home!"

He picked up his carrying pouch with determination and slung it over his shoulder.

He looked at her.

She had not moved.

Her small face was set and cold.

"You would do well to come with me. You will be safe with my people. Here there is nothing for you but pain and death."

She looked at him with her large eyes, but she gave no sign that she had changed her mind.

"I am going now," he said. "Are you coming?"

She shook her head.

"Goodbye."

She stared at him in silence.

"Thank you for saving my life."

He waited a few moments longer, but she did not move.

"Goodbye then," he said again and turned to go.

He looked back at her, but she still did not stir.

He started to walk, looking over his shoulder time and again, hoping she would follow him, not believing for a moment that she would not.

Deva often played tricks like this, but he always won in the end. She hated to be left alone and when she saw she was not going to get her own way she always gave in.

But Lark was not Deva.

Suddenly the dark smudge of her figure on the hill disappeared.

His heart leapt. She was coming.

But when some time had passed and there was no sign of her he was worried. He stopped where he was, standing in as much light as he could, hoping she would find him.

"Perhaps she is playing a trick on me and will stalk me in the shadows, making me think that she has gone the other way."

He still could not grasp that she would dare Na-Groth's country, alone.

He walked on, slowly, thinking to give her time to catch him up.

The night wheeled slowly past.

He strained to catch the smallest sound of breaking twig or rustling leaves that would betray her presence, but gradually it became clear to him that she was not going to join him.

With an exclamation of irritation he stopped in his tracks and sat down upon a boulder. He had to think.

A dark feeling of despair took over his heart. He was lonely, afraid, anxious. He did not know what to do.

All he knew was that the thing he most wanted to do, to go home, was somehow impossible.

He had never felt so lonely in his life.

He, who loved to be alone, was now lonely and afraid.

Almost without realizing he had made the decision, he stood up and turned on his heel.

He ran, clambering and scrambling over the moonlit screes, trying to retrace his steps to where he had last seen her.

When he came to the place where he thought they had slept, the shadows around him were different and he was not at all sure that it was the place after all.

He pressed on and on, the night riding beside him like his own shadow.

The pale glow of dawn found him deep into Klad with no sign or trace of Lark to comfort him.

Deva was not dead, but she lay in a coma so deep that all the healing arts of the Temple priesthood could not penetrate the dark shell that enclosed her.

Kyra watched by her bed until she was too weary to lift her hand in protest as Khu-ren carried her off to her sleeping rugs. Of all the powers she had, the skills she had developed in the long hard years of training, not one would come to her aid now that she most needed it.

Sitting beside her daughter, the only child she had or could ever have, her thoughts were dark and sad, weights holding down her winged spirit.

Gently Khu-ren reminded her of the dangers of an invasion from Klad and the urgency of their work with Isar to prevent it happening, but she could not listen. She understood the selfishness of Deva's love for Isar now. She experienced it herself. Nothing mattered to her if Deva died. And if Deva died it would be her fault. She had been too busy to realize how desperately her child had wanted Isar and how incapable she was of controlling that want. She should have helped her to understand, helped her to hold herself in check.

Tears flowed freely down her pale cheeks, worry gripped her mind like a cold hand, holding it immobilized so that she could not seek help from the deep inner levels of her consciousness, nor climb to the Spirit Realms to ask their help.

Khu-ren, loving them both, knew that there were things to be done. He had tried to use the power of the Inner Sanctum without Kyra's presence, but the place had been so disturbed by Deva's act of sacrilege, the great priest found himself curbed and limited.

The way the priests worked with the flow of energies from Nature had always been dependent on a subtle balance of their own spiritual vitality, concentration and respect.

No one *demanded* anything of the Spirit Realms.

No one carried his own desires into the Circle or took knowledge that was not freely given.

Khu-ren feared for Deva's life and sanity.

She had heard the Secret Name of Isar. She had spoken it loud and clear.

Would she be allowed to walk the earth again in the body of Deva, having that knowledge?

Would Isar suffer for it?

There was much a High Priest did not know, and Khu-ren sighed to think of it.

He went to a little wooden chest in which he and Kyra kept many precious things, and he took out the flake of chalk-stone stained brown with Deva's blood and scratched with the signs of his own country.

He read them aloud.

"The Spirit of Man is many . . ."

He pondered long and seriously.

Many summers ago Khu-ren had left the place of his birth, the Two Kingdoms of the Desert, fed by the Great River, and had come to Kyra's small forest country. In his own land he had been dissatisfied with the changes in the teaching of the Ancient Mysteries brought about by corrupt priests and kings who had forgotten how to be channels for the divine.

He had studied long and hard to reach his present position, dared initiation rites that had killed other men, learnt truths almost too heavy to bear, but during this time he had also grown in wisdom and sensitivity. He joined the secret Lords of the Sun and learned to travel the world in spirit form and commune with peoples he would never see in the flesh.

He had met Kyra in spirit form when she was an anxious child, frightened of the powers she had but did not yet understand. She came asking the mighty Lords of the Sun for help for her small, unsophisticated community in the far north of a green island country. A country which had no writing as his people knew it, but which read all natural things as though they were hieroglyphs. Trees, stones, the stars . . . all spelled out for them the words of their god.

Partly he had felt the natural pull of man to woman with this golden child, but more strongly he had felt the attraction of a new culture that seemed to answer all his doubts about his own.

Her people did not capture Truth in words, paint it on papyrus or hammer it on the rocks until it was so fixed and dead, it had nothing of itself left.

Truth for them was caught in flight, glancing from mind to mind. Always set free again. Never caged.

All their hidden resources of spirit were used to gain wisdom, and when a Truth was accepted it was accepted because it had been *experienced*, not because it was written down.

For many years after Khu-ren had met Kyra he was restless and undecided.

There was much that was great about his country, but he had a terrible foreboding of its end as he travelled the countryside and saw carved on every Temple wall static words, fixed and inflexible against change, monstrous texts boasting of royal deeds that never happened, glorifying war and killing, perpetuating the small thoughts of small minds for other small minds to

copy without understanding. Symbols of gods and spirits accepted as the gods and spirits themselves.

Kyra's country became for him a place to start
again, to try another way to Truth.

He had found it a hard way, exacting and uncom-
promising. But it had excited and satisfied him.

He knew that Deva had once, in another life, lived
in the country he had left, but he had not realized she
still visited it until he saw the stone she carved. Seeing
it had stirred old memories, old anxieties. In many
ways the country that was now his own would benefit
by writing. In many ways it would not. It had been an
issue he had considered long and seriously, and had
decided that their civilization was to be left to change
in its own way, in its own time. Neither he, nor Deva,
nor any of the carefully chosen students he had brought
with him would change the pace or nature of its slow
but subtle progress.

Was she there now, his daughter?

He turned the dusty stone over and over in his hand.

There was something else he knew about her past.

She and Isar had come to this country, immigrants
like himself, man and wife fleeing from their homeland
with a friend who had been threatened with execution.
They had lived in this very part of the country, before
the Great Temple had been built, and the man, who
was now Isar, had been murdered here. But he had

been born again many times since he had lived with Deva in those ancient times and had evolved, while Deva had taken her own life and refused to leave the place where he had been killed.

She had stayed, a shade, waiting for him, desperately clinging to her passion for him, refusing all change, all other destinies. It was she who chose Kyra to give her entrance to the time and place that would coincide with Isar's return.

The cord that bound them together was long and strong indeed.

Deva's eyelids stirred and Khu-ren stooped swiftly to massage her limbs.

How he longed to see into her mind!

Her long memories stretched to times before the corruption and her former father had been a man so great in wisdom that he had become a legend by the time Khu-ren was born.

Deva murmured something, but the word was unfamiliar to Khu-ren. A name perhaps? The name Isar had once been called?

Her eyelids were still again and she was lost to him.

Sadly he sat beside her until Kyra came to join him and then together they prayed for her return.

It was known by the priesthood of the Temple of the Sun that when a Stone had become defiled in some way and weakened in its power, there was a way of returning it to its former strength by certain rituals.

To begin with it was touched by the hands of priests

circling in the direction opposite to the normal one, as though unwinding an invisible cord from it, and then a visible cord was wound spiralling around it by the High Priest from ground level to tip and down again to ground level.

The cord was a special one, kept only for this purpose, in a stone jar with a lid, brought from over the sea in the ancient days.

It was made of three long and unbroken threads. One of the purest white wool, one of flax dyed with blue indigo, and one of fine gold wire. Where the cord had come from could no longer be remembered, but they all knew it was very precious and very sacred and must never be touched for purposes other than the Cleansing of the Stones. Prayers to accompany the winding process had been handed down by tradition, many of the words strange to the present priesthood, but intoned nevertheless with great care and reverence. There were some mysteries it was not wise to question. Belief had proved itself many times to be a powerful energy. Doubt was always destructive.

After the winding, came the unwinding, and the ceremonial return of the cord to the jar.

The cord and its beautiful container were then taken to the centre of the Circle of which the Stone was part, set upon the ground, three priests walking in measured steps around it, while drummers played an ancient tune, the beat of which was alien to the tunes of the usual Temple Ceremonies.

On this occasion it was not only one Sacred Stone that had been defiled, but the whole Inner Sanctum.

The ritual had to be repeated for each Stone of the Circle and three times for the three Stones that stood in the centre.

Beautiful the gold, the blue and the white.
Beautiful the Sun, the Sky and the Moon.

Beautiful the man who stands on the earth
and reaches to the Sun,
and reaches to the Sky,
and reaches to the Moon.

Beautiful is the Sun that speaks to Man of the
Source of All.
Beautiful is the Sky that speaks to Man of the Spirit
that encompasses All.
Beautiful is the Moon that speaks to Man of the
Earth that reflects the All.

Softly the reverberations of the drums and the ancient words wove their spell about the place.

Softly and subtly the light around them seemed to change.

The Storm

Isar journeyed deeper and deeper into danger searching for Lark.

Having been betrayed once he was cautious in his approach to other people, and it was not until he reached his third village that he was so tired and hungry he decided to risk showing himself.

He heard music coming from one of the houses and took this as a sign that the people had not yet been completely demoralized by Na-Groth's rule.

He slipped silently from the shelter of the woods and made for the house with music.

His heart ached for the old ways of his people, so suddenly changed. Now a man must look continually over his shoulder and on no day could he assume a tomorrow.

The music was sweet and sad, made partly by the

plucking of strings, partly by the blowing of pipes. He stood in the doorway and looked into the dim interior, his eyes slowly adjusting from blindness to shadowy sight.

To the people crowded into the house his presence brought fear and confusion. They were gathered about one of their number who had been brutally murdered by Na-Groth's men. They were secretly praying for him in the old way, which was now forbidden, and while they were doing so the light from the doorway was suddenly eclipsed, and the darkness of a long shadow fell upon them.

With his back to the light Isar's face could not be seen.

The music stopped.

For a long moment the air was heavy with shock and uncertainty, and then the son of the man who had been killed seized a heavy object and threw it with all his might at Isar's head. As it struck him with sickening force on the forehead he began to keel over and in that instant the man's son fell upon him with a howl of hate and beat him to the ground with all his strength.

In the darkness and confusion Isar tried to defend himself, but within moments other men had joined the boy and he was being kicked and punched from every direction. He was dimly aware of women screaming and men shouting, and then the pain of the blows upon him became too great and he fell into the deep hole of oblivion.

"He is dead!" one of the villagers said.

They stopped hitting him and drew back to look at him.

He was cut and bruised and bleeding, but in the light from the doorway they could now see he was not one of Na-Groth's men. His hair was long and the colour of copper, his skin pale and fine, his face and hands gentle and sensitive.

Another silence filled the house, different from the first.

"What have we done?" was in everyone's mind.

Killing had never been their way. Once the passion of anger had passed, they would have regretted this act even if it had been one of Na-Groth's men.

They took Isar in and brought water to wash his wounds.

They laid him beside the man whose funeral this had been, and begged his forgiveness for making the ceremony of his passing ugly with hatred and violence.

Isar lay still.

In a far country in a long ago time he remembered another boy who had been unjustly beaten, and lying in his cell, had waited for death. He had been freed by a young girl and her father.

She was with him now in a garden of great beauty, and he lay on thick grass with his head upon her lap. A pearl grey crane stooped to stalk a grasshopper close by them, and he could hear the soft hush of water falling from fountains. He wished time could stand still and this moment could last forever. Her hand was cool against his cheek. He could even feel the pulse in her wrist.

But time did not stand still and the crane, stretching its long, slender neck, flew away, as a voice called his name.

He heard it now as though it came from a great, great distance and he knew that there was something he must do. The girl's hands were holding him back. The voice was calling him away.

Struggling to regain consciousness Isar caught words the source of which he was not certain.

". . . you must leave the garden when you are ready . . . or the garden will leave you . . ."

Isar opened his eyes and looked into the anxious faces of strangers.

He lifted his hand to his head and felt the painful cuts and bruises.

"We are sorry," the people said humbly, "we thought you were one of Na-Groth's men."

"They killed my father," Gya, the young lad who had struck him first, explained.

"It is no matter," Isar said gently. "I should not have come upon you so suddenly. These are bad times."

"Bad times indeed," sighed several voices together.

"We are thankful you are not dead," someone said fervently.

Isar smiled faintly.

"So am I!"

The people laughed nervously and pressed food and

drink upon him, and propped him up with rolls of rugs so that his aching back would be supported.

He stayed a while with these people, his wounds being dressed tenderly, his every wish anticipated.

They hid him from the wandering bands of Na-Groth's men and found new clothes for him so that when it was time for him to move on he would not be so conspicuous.

The blow he had received on the forehead turned out to have been for the best after all. It left him with a scab that could almost pass for one of Na-Groth's marks.

"Why does he do this to people's foreheads?" Isar asked the woman who was dressing his wound, and who had commented that it would help him with his disguise.

She shrugged.

"It is the sacred place of the head, the Seeing place. In ancient times it is said that people had three eyes, and this is where the third one was. I do not know if that is true, but I have noticed that the priest used to place this part of his forehead against the Tall Stones of the Sacred Circle."

Isar looked thoughtful.

Na-Groth was symbolically blinding the conquered people as well as making them slaves.

In killing their priests he had truly blinded them, for the priests linked the community to the rest of the world and to the helpful Spirit Realms. Without them the community was limited and confined.

When the woman left him alone he prayed for help from Kyra and Khu-ren and the other mighty priests. His prayer was profound and sincere, but strangely seemed to make no contact.

His mind wandered to his mother and the man he accepted as his father, Karne. Their love still encompassed him and gave him comfort.

A small boy with straight ash white hair was sitting cross-legged on the floor of the chamber playing with pebbles, moving them around and talking softly to them as though they were people and he were acting out a story with them. Isar was sorry to break into his private world, but the thought of Fern had brought another thought with it.

He called to the child several times before his voice broke through the hold of his game.

At last he looked questioningly up at the tall stranger, with his innocent, wide blue eyes.

"Is there a Rowan tree near the Sacred Circle in this village?" Isar asked the boy.

The child stared at him.

"A Rowan tree?" Isar repeated.

The recognition in the boy's eyes showed that he knew what Isar was talking about, and that he knew where there was such a tree.

"Can you take me to it?" Isar pressed gently on.

Fear and darkness came to the boy's eyes and he shook his head vigorously.

"Why not?"

The boy did not answer, but Isar did not give up.

"Why not?"

"It is bad magic," he said.

"Nonsense!" cried Isar. He remembered when he was a child how on a certain day travellers had arrived from the North and were greeted with singing and joy because they brought the gift of a Rowan tree. It was carried in a leather bucket full of earth and was planted with joyful ceremony amongst the grove of Special trees the priests cultivated for medicinal and magical purposes.

"It is good magic!" he said to the boy.

The boy shook his head gloomily.

"Show it to me and I will tell you if it is good or bad magic."

The child looked at him intently as though trying to decide whether he could be trusted or not.

"You need not come near it yourself. Just show me where it is," wheedled Isar.

At last the boy agreed to help him.

Isar was weak and dizzy and had to lean upon his small shoulder. Haltingly they left the house and stumbled along a path half overgrown with brambles. It seemed a long way from the village, but when the child at last paused and pointed, Isar realized why he had been so afraid.

The Sacred Circle had been desecrated just as the first one he had seen in Klad had been, the rotting carcases of men were still hanging from the Stones, and a wave of such fearful evil wafted from it that Isar reeled back.

Not far from it grew the Rowan trees, but even they were mutilated and almost unrecognizable.

Na-Groth had evidently known something of their reputation.

The boy was cringing, his eyes big with horror.

"Go!" Isar cried, pushing him away, regretting that he had exposed him to this. "Go back to your home. I will try and change the bad magic to good magic."

"The Circle?" the boy whispered.

"No. That is beyond me. But I will try what I can do with the trees."

The boy retreated.

With a great effort of will Isar forced himself to go nearer the dread place, hoping that at least one of the trees was still alive.

Fern had told him once that all things were aware of each other in secret and subtle ways, time and space being no barrier to this kind of awareness. He knew that people could communicate in thought across the world, even though sometimes they did not realize they were doing it, but Fern had taught him that natural things could do this too. There was a Rowan tree in her garden and she had spent a great deal of time teaching him to know its ways.

"One day when you are in trouble, far from home, remember this tree. Find one of its kind and speak your heart to it. This one will hear it and bring me the message."

At the time he had not been sure that he believed her, but now he was in trouble, far from home, and he needed help.

He searched among the sad charred remnants of the

once beautiful trees, and found to his joy one pushing healthy shoots of green from scarred bark.

He stood beside it, holding the feathery leaves tenderly in his hand, stroking the deformed wood.

Deep in his being he called to Fern, told her of his danger and the suffering of the people he was amongst.

Then he stayed quiet for a long time, listening.

The air around him seemed to go very still and the boy who had retreated to the shelter of some bushes, but had not left him, fancied he could *feel* magic happening. His skin prickled cold and he looked around him apprehensively, but he was too curious to leave.

Slowly, Isar seemed to gain strength and comfort from the fresh life of the tree that had defied Na-Groth.

He could not say that he heard voices, but within himself he seemed to know what had to be done.

He was to find Lark and together they might have the strength and cunning to challenge Na-Groth and his god.

So be it.

He would not try to run away again.

As soon as he was fit enough to travel Isar set off, the villagers half sorry to see him go, half glad that they would no longer run the risk of hiding him.

The boy Gya, brown and lean and muscular, went with him, eager to help in any way he could. His mother and sisters watched him go and held back their tears until he was out of sight.

Danger was everywhere now and to walk into it with

head held high was no more foolhardy than to try to hide from it.

When they travelled the well-worn paths they kept careful watch for Na-Groth's men, but when they took to the forests there were other dangers. On the third day Isar narrowly escaped being gored by a wild boar. It was only Gya's presence of mind and skill with the boy that saved him.

That night they roasted boar steaks over their small fire and laughed about the incident, Gya much amused by the look of astonishment on Isar's face as the boar charged, and the clumsiness with which he fell about in the undergrowth trying to avoid the beast's tusks.

"You are good with that bow," Isar said with admiration. "Are you a hunter?"

"My father was. He taught me much. I used to go hunting with him sometimes, but more often than not we used to shoot just for the joy of it, not at living things, but at targets. Some of the boys would throw things in the air for us to aim at. My father never missed, but I cannot say the same for myself."

"I am glad you did not miss this time," Isar said with feeling.

Gya smiled.

"It is a matter of time and practice. I have had a bow so long it has become part of me. My father used to say that the bow is an extension of your arm, the arrow of your eye. It should become one action to look, to shoot and to hit. When I have shot well I feel I *am* the arrow. When I do not feel this I know I am going to miss the mark."

"Do you not feel pity for the life you end when your arrow reaches a living creature?"

Gya's brown eyes clouded slightly.

"I do not shoot for the pleasure of killing. I shoot to keep alive—and to save life!" he added, looking reproachfully at Isar.

Isar acknowledged the rebuff and bowed his head slightly.

The meat was good and he was very hungry.

As they came nearer to Na-Groth's stronghold, they kept more and more under cover and asked fewer questions of the villagers they met.

Eyes became increasingly unfriendly and wary, words were short and unwelcoming, fields were unworked, children thin and hungry. The men were mostly away, busy with Na-Groth's work, and the women and children were left to tend the land. In normal times this would not have been so disastrous as the women and children had always worked side by side with the men in anything that needed doing, but now the will to work had gone. Whatever they made or grew was taken from them. They were lonely, afraid and resentful. They could no longer feel the presence of invisible helpers, no longer believe that everything they did had meaning and purpose.

Na-Groth had told them the Spirit Realms did not exist.

They were alone but for Na-Groth and his fearsome god.

So shaken was Gya by what he had seen and heard,

that he railed against their ancient God that he should
let such monsters as Na-Groth exist and flourish.

Isar was silent at first, remembering how recently he
had felt the same way, but thoughts were struggling to
take shape and he felt bound to share them with Gya.

"You cannot drink from a stagnant pool without
being sick," he said. "The clear stream fed by a
healthy spring is constantly moving, fighting obstruc-
tions, changing and causing change. Do you not see,
Gya, our way of life was good, but if it were never
challenged, it would become stagnant?"

Gya had come to respect Isar in the time they had
been together. At first he had been amused that Isar
knew so little about the things that came easily to himself, but now he was beginning to see that physical
prowess was not the only defence against evil.

"Our God gives us the dignity of free choice. Na-
Groth chooses one way, and we another. *Ours* is the
responsibility, and it is *our* efforts that will have to set
the wrong to rights. Do you not see that?"

Gya could feel Isar's convictions strengthening his
own. He felt inspired to leap up and attack the armies
of Na-Groth single handed.

"No," laughed Isar. "That is not the way. No man
has enough arrows to kill the armed men of Groth.
They will spring up again as fast as they are killed if
the idea that feeds them is not first discredited. We
must use our minds before we use our arms in this
battle."

The two young men sat together on the hill,

shadowed by trees, the sun sloping to the Western horizon, where dark clouds rose to meet it.

They sat silently for a long time, Isar deep in thought, Gya flicking little bits of twig at a particular stone. Even at rest he was flexing and training his muscles and his eyes to accuracy of aim.

The night brought heavy rains and harsh winds.

Karne, making his way westwards, was gathering fighting men to his side.

"I do not say that we *will* have to fight, but we will form a barrier as long as is needed between the troubled land of Klad and our own houses. This will give the priesthood of our Temple time to work their magic on the enemy and drive it from our shores."

The story of Panora's war had become legend, and the defeat of a mighty army, on the plains not far from the Great Temple itself, by the sole use of priestly Mysteries, was told around the cooking fires from one end of the country to the other.

The people had great faith in their priesthood and Karne did not choose to tell them that the priests of the Tall Stones and the Sacred Circles in Klad had been destroyed as easily as ordinary men.

Not all the men he spoke to joined him on the march, but enough to make a sizeable force grew steadily as they approached the menace in the west.

Villagers near to Klad were already in a state of agitation. Friends and relatives had disappeared on market journeys to the west. They were beginning to realize that something was very wrong, but had not been sure what it was.

The night of storm and rain that beset Isar and Gya on their hill doused the cooking fires of Karne's army and hid their approach from Na-Groth's spies.

In the Temple of the Sun the Sacred Inner Sanctum was gradually restored to power. Kyra could feel the coursing and the spiralling of its energy as she leant her forehead to the Stones.

"Now," she called in a ringing voice, "let us begin!"

The priests took their positions around the Circle, the two Lords of the Sun stood within the triangle of the Holy Three at the centre.

"Now!" Khu-ren cried, and as the wind of the coming storm rose soughing in the trees, the sound of their incantation rose to meet it.

Round and round the priests went, stirring the invisible energies of the air.

Still stood the two tall Lords of the Sun, male and female, concentrating their energy and their will to reach Isar in a distant and desolate land.

In her garden Fern stood with her arms around her Rowan tree, her cheek against its trunk, which pulled against her, as above, its branches were torn and buffeted by the wind.

She thought of Karne and Isar, and prayed that all the strength of the Spirit Realms there to help them would be wisely used.

"Remember," she whispered, "you are not alone. No one is alone. Remember it!"

Deva's eyelids flickered and for the first time since she had fallen into unconsciousness she opened her eyes and looked around her.

She was alone in Kyra's chamber, the flame of a lamp flickering beside her, the sound of wind and rain howling and beating against the wooden walls of the house, the door covering flapping like the wings of a trapped bird.

Slowly she sat up, looking around her at the shadows, everything unfamiliar. Where was the hot sand of the desert, the green lush lands of the flood plain of the Great River, and her father's Pyramid gleaming in the sun?

Slowly her eyes adjusted as her mind accepted what she saw.

She knew that she was Deva, the daughter of Khuren and Kyra.

The storm drove Isar and Gya to shelter under a ledge of rock, squeezed between the rough earth and the hard stone, their hands scratched from the bushes and plants they had pulled aside in their haste as the wind drove a sudden squall of rain upon them.

As the night wore on the two young men fell uneasily into dark pits of sleep, only to find themselves, unrefreshed, struggling to wakefulness again. So savage was the night Isar found himself fearing that it would go on forever, that Groth had somehow extinguished the God of Light, and nothing but darkness and despair was left to contemplate.

It was during one of these moments of half sleep that Isar was startled to see the dark outline of a figure standing on the hillside beside him.

Illuminated in the sudden splendour of a flash of lightning he recognized the Lady Kyra.

He gasped and struggled to free himself from the encumbrance of the branches and turfs he had laid upon himself.

"My lady!" he cried and wrenched himself free, half tumbling out of the cleft of rock into the stinging night.

But she was gone.

The next lightning flash revealed a hillside empty save for the thin trees struggling in the clutches of the wind and a distraught Isar streaming with icy water.

"What are you doing?" shouted Gya. "Have you gone mad?"

"The Lady . . . I saw the Lady Kyra," Isar babbled frantically, searching into the darkness for the figure he had seen so briefly but so tantalisingly close.

"There is no one there. You are crazy!" growled Gya. "Come back before you fall and break your neck."

Isar looked around him as lightning flooded the scene once more with its eery, sickly light.

There was nobody there.

Gya was right. He was crazy.

He crawled back under the ledge, shivering and soaked, his heart aching with disappointment.

"Rub yourself, beat your arms . . . you will freeze to death if you do not."

Gya began to pummel him and he rubbed himself as best he could with his stiff, icy hands. Warmth came gradually to him, but sleep was gone and for the rest of the night they talked, Isar telling Gya about his home and the Temple of the Sun, and the woman he thought he had seen on the hillside.

"From what you say," Gya said, "it is quite possible she was there . . . in spirit form I mean."

"Which means . . ." Isar's face lit up. "We are not alone and lost. They know where we are and will help us."

Gya slapped him on the back.

"That is good news indeed, and I will tell you some more!"

"What is it?"

"Listen."

"I am listening."

"Does it not seem quieter to you? The storm has almost passed."

Isar was so thankful, he did not reply, but buried his head on his knees to say a prayer of gratitude. He was so cold and wet, he did not think he could endure much more of such a night.

As he shut his eyes he seemed to see the Temple and its priests around him, faintly, as one sees an after image, fading even as he tried to hold it. The Lord Khu-ren's face was the last to disappear and Isar could see his mouth moving, but he could not make out what the words were.

Gya was shaking his shoulder.

"First light is on its way," he said urgently. "We should move. We will never be dry and warm until we do."

Isar was so dazed and unresponsive, Gya took the initiative and hauled his friend up by the arm and pushed him into the open.

Isar looked around him. The first greyness of dawn was giving shape slowly and imperceptibly to the landscape. The wind had already dropped and the rain was falling only lightly.

They gathered their few belongings together, Gya tenderly testing the gut string of his bow and rubbing it with fat from a small pouch, before he was prepared to move.

Shuddering and shivering with cold they set off down the hill away from the rising light. When they reached flat ground they started to run, rejoicing in the warmth the exercise gave them.

The visions Isar had seen had given him courage. He had begun to feel there was no way out of Groth's dark clutches, but now he knew he was wrong.

The Sun was not dead.

"And even if the Sun did die," Isar thought, "what is the sun but one form of created light? The Source of All, the Creator, is still there."

Groth could only at his most powerful put out the light of one small sun. He could not challenge the Whole, for he himself was only a small part of the whole.

Comforted, Isar began to make plans.

He saw Gya and himself, the saviours of a whole people, striding down into Na-Groth's dark domain, challenging him . . . Gya felling him with one swift arrow, while Isar of the silver tongue made speeches to the cowed populace and renewed their faith in the old ways.

He caught himself smiling as he jogged along.

He saw his triumphant return home and Deva running to meet him, excited by the stories she had heard of his victory. He saw his mother putting a garland of leaves about his head, and Karne, the great Spear-Lord, bowing to him.

There would be a festival of thanksgiving and Gya and he would be honoured guests, taken to the very heart of the Temple.

"What are you laughing at?" Gya's voice broke through his dream.

"O . . . nothing," Isar replied, flushing slightly, glad that Gya could not see into his thoughts.

"I see the rain has soaked into your head and your thoughts are floating in it," Gya said sourly. "I will have to do the thinking for both of us."

This pulled Isar up short.

"I am sorry, friend," he said soberly. "I was floating as you say, but now I am on dry land. How far do you think we are from Na-Groth?"

"Not far. We had better avoid all tracks and villages."

The dim light of a grey damp day was around them. The landscape was sodden and heavy, as though from prolonged weeping.

"Poor earth," Isar thought, "she feels the tread of Na-Groth's feet as heavily as the people do."

"You are thinking again!" accused Gya.

Isar had a way of withdrawing into himself from time to time that disturbed Gya. He could not follow and he could not understand. He himself never felt the need to retreat from the world. He was always present, always eager to sample what it had to offer and to test his skills against it.

Fear and despair were not feelings that came easily to Gya, though he had known them briefly when his father died. Deep thoughts about the meaning of life were also rare for him.

He listened with interest to Isar's description of the Temple and the beliefs that sustained it. He knew there were many in his village who shared these beliefs even though Na-Groth had worked hard and harshly to destroy them. But for his own part he was prepared to leave the Ultimate Question unanswered and busy himself with matters of more immediacy.

When he had said this to Isar, his friend had been shocked.

"But you cannot separate the two," he had cried, "awareness of the total shape of things affects the way you live your life. A traveller walking through a marsh treads differently from one climbing a rocky mountain, and a man going nowhere treads differently from a man going somewhere."

Gya could not deny it.

"I will think about it, one day," he said, "but now all that I can think about is finding Na-Groth."

The two young men journeyed on, keeping to the wild places, but always bearing to the west.

By midday the sun was breaking through the clouds in fitful patches, and their bodies told them that they were hungry.

Fern's training had given Isar a wide knowledge of plants, and it was Isar, the dreamer, who provided their meal, while Gya, the hunter, came back empty handed from his search for food.

"I am glad to see you are good for something in this world," teased Gya.

Isar punched him and laughed to see him roll with exaggerated movements and much hilarity down the slope he had just climbed up.

"Catch," he called down to him and threw a bundle of edible leaves and roots after him.

And so it was that Gya was halfway down the hill, and obscured by bushes, when Na-Groth's men suddenly appeared and seized Isar.

The Capture

When Kyra and Khu-ren returned to their home early in the morning after the storm, they found Vann, the healer-priest, with Deva. She was sitting up and sipping broth from her favourite earthenware bowl, made by Kyra when she was a young girl.

The weariness that made Kyra ache in every limb, lifted, the instant she saw her daughter so recovered.

"Deva!" she cried and flung her arms around her, tears she had kept back all night welling from her eyes and falling on the girl's dark hair.

Khu-ren stood beside them, no less relieved and pleased, though he did not show it quite so openly.

"I have good news for you, my love." Kyra was smiling through her tears.

Deva who had coldly held herself back from her

mother's embrace now turned to her, her eyes blazing with the question she dared not ask.

"No. He is not back, but he is safe and we have seen him." Kyra said. "He has a friend with him. No, I do not know who it is, but there were two young men sheltering from a storm, and one of them was Isar. He saw me for an instant, but the air was too wild with lightning fire for the vision to hold steady. But we know where he is and he knows we are giving him support. Everything will be much easier now."

Deva buried her face against her mother's breast and sobbed.

"I miss him so!"

"I know. It will not be long."

Khu-ren took his daughter's hands and turned her slightly away from her mother.

"Where have you been?" he asked quietly, but in a tone that carried authority.

Deva did not answer.

"Not now my lord," Kyra said gently. "Not now! Is it not enough that she is back with us?"

The Lord Khu-ren straightened and looked down upon the girl thoughtfully, and then he drew Kyra aside to speak to her privately.

"It is not good to let her escape to the past all the time. She will never learn to grow with this life and be ready for the next."

"But surely not now! There will be time enough to discuss these matters with her when Isar is safely home again."

Khu-ren's face looked dark and doubtful.

"Who knows what time we have left," he said somberly. "Now is the best time for everything."

"I beg of you," Kyra whispered. "She is not strong. See how pale she is."

The girl indeed was pale, her black eyes and black hair startling against the pallor of her skin.

"She needs rest," Vann now spoke for her and because Khu-ren had great respect for him as friend and healer, he allowed himself to be persuaded.

"Let her rest then," he said briefly, "but watch her well and do not let her drift away again."

Vann nodded, and wiped the girl's damp face with a soft cloth he had by him.

Kyra sat down beside her, enfolding her in her embrace and rocking her slightly backwards and forwards as though she were a very young child again.

The Lord Khu-ren watched them for a while, his face tender and loving, though there was still a line of anxiety between his brows. Then he left the room and sought sleep for himself elsewhere.

The weariness that had temporarily left Kyra when she saw Deva was so much better, returned, and her limbs grew heavy and her eyelids longed to close. Vann, seeing this, gently moved the rugs around the two women so that they were warm and together, and together they drifted into sleep.

Before he left the chamber Vann leant down and listened to Deva's breathing. He was content that she was deep in natural sleep and not in trance.

As they slept it was the mother who slipped back in time, but to memories not far distant from the present, to her life as a child in a far northern community amongst heather and rocks, a circle of Tall Stones upon a hill which was the testing ground of a friend called Maal, and an enemy called Wardyke.

At midday the two women woke, Deva forming a question even as Kyra emerged from the dream.

"My lady, who is Maal? I sense great love for him in the way you call upon him in your sleep."

Kyra woke slowly, sleep falling from her like soft mist from a hill warmed by the sun. But she seemed to be still part mist, part woman, listening for something, stretching her senses to catch something Deva could not hear.

Deva waited with patience beside her, but after a while Kyra seemed to stop trying to hear the inaudible and see the invisible.

"Maal was the priest of my village before I came here," she said. "Karne, Fern and I loved him greatly. He taught us to see in ways we did not think it possible to see, and hear in ways we did not think it possible to hear."

There was a sad catch to Kyra's voice.

"You speak of him in the past," Deva said. "Did he die?"

"Yes, he died."

Kyra was listening again, a frown of concentration gathering on her forehead.

"What is it?" Deva whispered. "What do you hear?"

"I do not know. It is just that . . . it may have been the dream that brought him back so vividly to my mind that I think I hear his voice . . . or perhaps he brought

the dream to me . . . He promised me . . ." Her voice
trailed away in silent memories.

"What did he promise you?"

"He promised to come back to me when I really
needed him. And now . . ." Kyra stood up with sudden conviction. "There could not be a time I needed
him more!"

Deva was wide eyed.

"Do you think he is alive?"

"Alive yes—but on what level I do not know."

"How will you know him if he has come back?"

"I will know," Kyra said confidently, and then
laughed. "He always used to say "You will know when
the time comes," and it annoyed me! I always asked
for explanations, signs, proofs, but he would never give
them to me. And yet he proved right every time. I *did*
know when the right moment had come for things that
he foretold. And I know now, somewhere, somehow,
he is trying to reach me."

Kyra's beautiful face was alight with joy and hope.

"I long to meet him," said Deva, a shade envious of
her mother's love for him.

"Maybe you will!" Kyra cried. "Come child, let us
comb your hair and wash your face. Make yourself
bright for the new day. Everything will be better now
that Maal is near!"

Gya watched helplessly as the brutal warriors of Groth
beat Isar and dragged him down the other side of the
hill and out of sight.

His first instinct was to seize his bow and his arrow and let fly at them, but foolishly he had laid them down beside Isar when he had returned from the hunt. The men had taken them.

He knew that it would be hopeless to try to fight unarmed. He was heavily outnumbered.

He stayed hidden, his heart pounding with frustration, and decided that the only thing he could do was to follow and see where they took Isar.

It was strange that they had not killed him outright. They must have received orders about him.

Gya crept as silently and as swiftly as he could around the base of the hill, guided by the sounds the men were making as they crashed through the long grass and the bushes. They were shouting to each other in their guttural foreign tongue and some of them were singing a sombre song.

Gya came near enough to ascertain that Isar was still with them and still alive, and then he kept well back and out of sight. His thoughts were bitter with regret that he had left his bow unattended.

He would get it back whatever the cost, and he would rescue his friend!

But meanwhile he needed patience and skill at keeping hidden. His hunting experience helped him greatly and Na-Groth's men caught no scent of him.

After several pauses to drink at streams, and once to terrorize a village and demand food, the group began

to climb a steep ridge and make for a cleft that seemed
to offer easier passage.

Gya was still with them, weary and scratched and
desperately hungry, but the sight of Isar, bound and
staggering and constantly beaten, kept him going.

Half way up the ridge he realized with dismay that
the pass was heavily guarded.

This gave him pause, and, for a moment, he thought
he would have to turn back, but his friend and bow
were in the hands of the enemy and were being carried
inexorably nearer to the stronghold of the dread Na-
Groth. He was determined that he would not desert
them.

Keeping close in the wake of Isar's captors, he
passed the guards unseen while they were still joking
and shouting friendly insults at each other. He was so
close to the bird of danger that he could hear its heart
beat.

Pausing at the lip of the ridge overlooking the plain
to the west, Gya could scarcely refrain from gasping.

Night was close to falling and its dark stain was already over the land below, although the ridge was still
in light.

As far as he could see the natural green of the earth
had been destroyed. Ragged black tents and shabby
wooden shacks were sprawling everywhere, cooking
fires were so numerous it almost seemed that the whole
plain was smouldering, and a suffocating lid of smoke
hovered over the place, cutting off fresh light and air
from the inhabitants.

Gya wondered if they ever saw the sky and mar-
velled at the stars.

Hastily he ducked behind some hawthorn bushes as
the guards and Isar's captors finished their fraternizing.

Gya wondered what Isar was thinking as he lifted
his head to look at the scene below.

He must have been in despair.

Na-Groth's people outnumbered the people of the
villages many times, and nothing held them back from
cruelty and killing. Their leader preached it. Their god
demanded it. It was difficult to keep in mind that they
were also human, and so subject to natural laws of
change.

Gya knew that he could not afford to lose sight of
Isar now. Amongst those innumerable hovels it would
be impossible to find him.

He kept close, silent as a wild cat stalking its prey,
glad of the falling dark.

Isar's captors lit torches and their acrid smell and
guttering flames led Gya on. It was completely dark by
the time they reached their destination.

Drawn back in the shadows, Gya stared aghast at
the vast palace of Na-Groth, its wooden columns hung
with skulls, flickering white in the light of the fires that
burned on the open ground before it.

In the centre of this open space stood a giant figure.

The hateful Na-Groth himself.

Gya shuddered and drew back.

Isar was dragged before the palace of Na-Groth and pushed down upon his knees.

The leader of his captors shouted and struck his spear loudly upon the ground.

From the dark chasm of the entrance a man appeared, robed in red, the colour of death.

Isar could see his eyes glittering in the flame light and his cheeks shadowed and hollowed like a skull's.

He carried a tall staff and thumped it on the earth imperiously.

Dust rose.

He spoke words Isar did not understand and was answered in the same language.

Isar was hauled up and pushed forward, so that he fell on his knees in front of the man.

His mind told him to rise, his pride as a free being cried out against the indignity of kneeling to this creature, but his body was weak from the rigours of the day and it would not obey his command.

The man, noting the struggle in the boy's face, smiled, and the smile was the most chilling thing Isar had ever seen.

"Come!" he said suddenly in Isar's language, but with a stranger's intonation.

The soldiers pulled Isar to his feet and pushed him to follow the robed figure. In the darkness of the monstrous building he struggled to think of ways of escape, but his weariness robbed him of all his initiative.

The passage, dimly lit by an occasional sputtering torch, gave way at last to a huge chamber, where impotent and lifeless trees formed the columns that held the roof of wood and hides high above them.

All the wood in the building had been charred and polished in some way so that it had a dull, dark gleam.

Fires in small stone enclosures were burning at intervals around the hall, and torches were leaning from the columns above the height of a man's head. The atmosphere was hot and thick with a sickly sweet smell. Near the roof, the smoke gathered and hung oppressively.

At the end of the chamber and focussed in most of the light, Na-Groth and his Queen sat on high thrones of the same dark polished timber.

Isar was led before them and, again, given a push from behind that precipitated him on his knees before his enemy.

The man who had brought him spoke long and eloquently. Although Isar could not understand the words, he caught the boasting drift of it. It seemed that he had been specially sought and that his capture was regarded as a great achievement.

Fleetingly he wondered why this was so, but had no time to think the question through.

All his effort was concentrated on bringing himself to his feet.

He was bound and his body weary to desperation, but he was determined not to kneel to Na-Groth.

Around him the court of Na-Groth was gathered, warriors and guards, old men in long robes like the one who had greeted him at the entrance, women in garments the like of which he had never seen and, behind the Queen, two lines of young girls, her personal attendants.

The Queen was magnificent in form, her hair sloe black but her skin pale. Her eyes were like black diamonds and it was she who commanded his first attention. It was the curl of her lip that goaded his flagging strength to one last effort.

Clumsily he staggered to his feet.

"Kneel before the great Na-Groth and his Queen!" commanded the skull-faced man, pointing his staff at him, his eyes blazing.

But Isar stood precariously on his feet, lifting his chin and daring to look directly into the eyes of the deadly Queen, and then into those of Na-Groth. There he met such a look of crazed greed that he almost reeled back. The man was either drugged or mad. His eyes were blurred and bloodshot, but the muscular hand that gripped the side of his throne was endowed with almost superhuman strength.

Isar had the feeling in those few crowded moments that Na-Groth was not in charge of himself.

Someone, or something, else, ruled his dark soul.

Isar looked back to the Queen.

Was it she?

But he did not think so.

Both of them were looking out from the dark holes of their eyes, using the splendour of their surroundings to hide their own inadequacy.

Kyra could command respect and speak with author-

ity, standing barefoot in a field, with nothing more than
a peasant's loose woollen shift about her.

But these people had to use tricks to give them
stature.

The skulls, the fires, the dark wood, the towering
columns, even the use of giant shadows in the spaces
between the columns, were all part of the illusion.

The warriors' swords and spears, however, were
real, and he had felt the harshness of their knuckles.

He thought back to the Temple of the Sun and
asked for strength to outface his enemies.

Behind the Queen's throne he noticed a slight movement and turned his eyes towards it.

His heart leapt.

Lark was there, her deep, expressive eyes willing
him to silence.

Joy at seeing her was extinguished instantly in anxiety for her safety as well as for his own. He knew
without any doubt that she was there because she was
forced to be there. Most of the other attendants looked
as though they had come to accept the advantages of
their situation, but Lark's eyes had not changed since
he had seen her last, and he knew she was still loyal to
the old ways and the overthrow of Na-Groth's power.

He looked away from her, knowing that he must
give no sign that he recognized her, or she too would
be lost.

"Kneel!" the command was given again, harshly.

He stood his ground.

A guard whipped him until he at last fell down.

"I see . . ." he managed to bring out from his

bleeding mouth, "Na-Groth does not want the respect of free men, only the fear of slaves!"

This time the whipping he received made him lose consciousness.

The Invisible Enemy

Karne was hoping to keep his small army well hidden from Na-Groth. Surprise was his greatest strength, for the men he had with him were greatly outnumbered and, most of them, unused to conflict.

But Na-Groth was no fool.

Even as Isar lay bound and bleeding on the floor of one of the dark chambers of the palace, and Karne was surveying his men and speaking to them of surprise, one of Na-Groth's spies was kneeling before the two thrones and speaking of the puny force the Temple had managed to muster.

Na-Groth laughed hugely at the description.

"So be it!" he roared, still laughing. "If they want to

die as heroes, let them die as heroes! We will not disappoint them."

The place was filled with the noise of people stamping their feet in approval and Na-Groth's humourless and rasping laughter.

It was the Queen who raised her hand at last for silence, and on the instant, everyone froze as though a sudden chill wind had swept over them.

She glared at everyone in front of the thrones, her venomous eyes subduing them, compelling them to their knees.

When the whole vast hall was full of silent, kneeling figures, she rose to her feet, drawing her lord with her.

The two stood on their dark platform, high above their subjects.

Na-Groth was not laughing now and his face was gathering darkness like the sky before a storm.

He waited long enough for the silence to become intolerable and then he raised his fist above his head and brought it down like an axe, his voice spitting out the words:

"Crush them like flies!"

"Like flies!" screamed his minions at his feet.

"Like flies," said his Queen with satisfaction in her cold and deadly voice.

"Let the beacon fires be lit and the warriors be sent!" roared Na-Groth.

It was as though a dark wind swirled through the hall and gathered all the people up like winter leaves.

No one but Na-Groth and his lady Maeged remained.

Khu-ren and Kyra were very near to despair.

For all their skill they could not reach Isar.

The black malevolence of Na-Groth's rule produced powerful vibrations, stronger as they centred on the persons of Na-Groth and Maeged.

Their palace was impregnable to the priests of Light.

Khu-ren, in spirit-travel, could visit the ridge that overlooked the encampment and could see quite clearly the distant dark palace, but, when he tried to move towards it, the air broke up around him in swirling currents, and he had to use all his psychic strength not to be sucked down into the vortex of Na-Groth's destructive will.

"We need someone inside the palace to reach out to us," he explained to Kyra.

"If only Isar were strong enough!" she said sadly.

Khu-ren looked at her closely and his voice took on the tenderness of warning.

"You must prepare yourself, my love," he said gently.

"For what?"

She looked at him with frightened eyes, for she knew the answer.

"Isar may be dead."

"No!" she cried.

"It would be surprising if he were not. We have lost contact with him completely, which means either he is dead already, or he is well within the range of Na-Groth's power. We could not expect that Na-Groth would not have killed him as soon as he found him."

Kyra was silent, her shoulders bent and her face desolate.

Khu-ren put his arm around her and they sat together, deep in thought.

Gradually Kyra began to straighten up and pull away from her husband.

She had that look upon her face that she had when she was listening for something ordinary ears could not catch.

He drew back at once and waited beside her, hardly daring to move in case he disturbed her concentration.

Slowly . . . slowly she turned to her husband.

"What is it?" he whispered.

"It is Maal," she said, her voice shaking, "I am sure it is Maal!"

He kissed her and held her tight.

"Where is he?"

"I do not know . . . the impression was very faint and strange. There was a girl and he was a shadow behind the girl . . . and his voice came from the mouth of the girl . . . and yet . . . and yet I did not get the impression they were the same person . . ."

Kyra strained to recapture the experience, but it was gone.

"What did he say?"

"Karne . . . is . . . in danger. His position is known to Na-Groth. There was something about flies . . . but I did not understand that."

"Never mind what you did not understand. We have enough to know that Karne is in danger, and him, at least, we *can* reach.

"Come."

He took her hand and they prepared again for the adventure of spirit-travel.

Karne posted the watches for the night and took one of the positions himself.

He was restless and knew that he would not be able to sleep though his body was weary from the effort of the day. At times he felt it was only the strength of his own will that sustained this crowd of men and drove them away from their families and into danger.

It was not an easy burden to bear.

Up to now his determination to gather an army and move it to Klad had kept him going.

But now they were in position as near to Na-Groth as they dared to be, he was not sure what to do next. He did not want to fight if it could be avoided.

On their way he had made constant inquiry of villagers about the passage of a tall, red-haired youth, and was convinced from what he had heard that Isar was too far ahead of them for their paths to cross.

He sat in the darkness, watching over his men, and thinking anxiously about Isar.

He looked up into the clear sky above him, and it was as though a sudden reversal of his normal thinking occurred.

From being Karne, master of his own actions, leader of men, proud Spear-Lord on whose shoulders rested the cares of his people, he had become a minute point in an immensity of Nothing.

Confidence in himself, his people, his god, trickled

away. He felt as though a suffocating black cord had settled round his chest and was somehow drawing tighter and tighter.

At first he abandoned himself to the desperation of the experience, and then his old habits of thinking and believing began to return.

He broke from the clutches of despair and shook his head fiercely to clear it of its dark thoughts.

He thought of his sister, younger than himself, but often wiser.

"Help me," he cried deeply in himself. "I cannot see the way!"

Was it possible there *was* no way?

"Karne!"

He heard his name called and turned his head.

Kyra was standing before him, faintly luminous in the darkness.

He sprang up and made to move towards her.

"No!" she said sharply, holding up her slender white hand.

For a moment she seemed to disappear and Karne felt a choking lump rising in his throat.

"Fool!" he cursed himself.

But she returned, and this time he remained as motionless as the still night air.

"Listen to me . . . there is no time . . . Na-Groth knows you are here . . . Try to . . ."

But before she could complete the sentence the noisy approach of one of the men complaining that he had watched long enough and was ready to sleep broke the tenuous thread of the vision.

Kyra was gone.

Karne rounded angrily on the man.

"No one will sleep tonight," he roared, "wake everybody up!"

"What?" gasped the fellow, staring stupidly.

"You heard me! Wake everybody up and tell them to report to me at once."

As the oaf still stared and gaped, Karne punched him in the chest.

"Move!" he shouted. "We are about to be attacked!"

This made the man move.

While the men, confused and grumbling, were gathering around him, Karne was planning.

All doubts of purpose and meaning were gone.

He enjoyed action, and action they were about to have.

Meanwhile Gya, who was hiding among the hovels of Na-Groth's encampment, was needing all his cunning to stay alive, and had not yet found a way to reach his friend in the Palace or retrieve his bow.

He had managed to steal some food and was sitting in the dark shadow of an untidy pile of wood, when he had the sensation that he was being watched. His hands went automatically to his weapons before he remembered that he no longer had them.

He stayed tensely still and looked carefully around him.

At first he saw no one and then there was a slight movement to the left.

Turning his head swiftly he looked into the watching

shadow of a small girl. She seemed no more than seven or eight summers old and so thin and sickly it was not likely that she would see the ninth.

He crept towards her holding out what was left of the meat he had stolen earlier from an unguarded spit.

She did not move back in fear as he half expected her to do, but continued, unmoving, to stare at him.

Her scrutiny began to make him feel uneasy.

He was shocked to see her face and limbs were marked with festering sores.

For the first time Gya felt great pity for these people, particularly for the children, who were caught in a trap as surely as were his own people.

There was no malevolence in the eyes of the child as she stared at him, only curiosity.

"Here," he said softly. "Take this. Eat."

He imitated the motions of putting the meat to his mouth and eating, and then he held it out to her.

Briefly her eyes left his and moved to the meat, and then back again to his.

"It is yours. Eat," he whispered.

Whether she would have taken it or not he would never know, because a woman's voice called out "Berka!" and instantly she turned and ran.

Gya was in a quandary.

He was not sure if the child would give him away or not, but he could not risk it.

He must move.

He stuffed the last of the food hungrily into his mouth and looked around for somewhere new to hide.

It was late and most of the fires had died down.

There were more dark places than before in which to hide, but also more risk of tripping over or bumping into something.

By this time of the night his own people would have been soundly asleep, but a great many of Na-Groth's people seemed to be still awake.

Groups of them were gathered, drinking barley ale. Their laughter came in strangely regular little bursts, as though the laughter had nothing to do with the way they felt, but was expected of them.

Others were wandering about, poking around other people's cooking fires, as though hoping to pick up left-overs. He saw one or two find something and instantly pounce on it, looking furtively from side to side.

They did not see him.

One ate whatever it was, and then slithered away into the shadows, while the other hid what he had found in his clothes, and ran from the place.

Gya smiled wryly to himself.

Who would have thought he, swift, proud Gya the bowman, would have become a nocturnal scavenger no better than these other human dogs?

Again a fleeting ripple of pity touched his heart.

Had these people once been as carefree and as kindly as his own people had been?

His face darkened.

He remembered how he had attacked Isar, a harmless stranger.

Was Groth's dark taint already upon them?

Just before the first light of dawn, Na-Groth's warriors

crept up upon the position their spies had given them for Karne's motley army. They could see the humped shapes of sleeping figures, just faintly where they showed against the sky, or in the last dying glow from the watch fires.

Swiftly they moved, their weapons ready.

Clubs were raised, axes and knives lifted to position above unsuspecting bodies.

No sound was made.

The leader held his breath for one long and fateful moment and then, with a short, sharp exhalation, plunged his blade into the first of the sleeping figures.

Instantly his men were about their grizzly work.

No one was spared.

Violence and hate had won.

Strangely the enemy did not fight back.

No sound came from the camp.

Na-Groth's men would have expected some screams and groans, if not resistance.

Could they have killed the whole army in one instant?

Na-Groth's captain stood up and stared into the dark.

His men stood poised and uneasy.

Not sure what they had done.

Not sure what there was still to do.

And as they listened, they began to hear, fine and eery, a high pitched note, that seemed at first so faint that it could have been one of their own body-sounds, and then, gradually, gradually becoming so strong that they were aware of it outside themselves, and everywhere surrounding them . . . above them . . . in the air . . . in the sky . . .

It was unearthly.

It was nothing they had heard before.

It chilled their hearts.

Some flailed about with weapons trying to find the source, but there seemed to be no source.

The sound was everywhere in equal intensity . . . strange, thin, hollow, inhuman . . . It seemed to pervade the universe, and grow stronger every instant.

The warriors who had been so bold and confident, part of a well disciplined unit, began to break up in panic.

Each man suddenly seemed to be alone, in the dark, with some mysterious and unknown force homing in on him.

Terrified, Na-Groth's rabble scattered, stumbling and fleeing, the sound pursuing them, rising in pitch, until it seemed to be the sound of mockery and of triumph.

Above them the sky slowly reddened, appearing menacing to Na-Groth's men, but friendly to the men of Karne who were merry as they climbed down from the trees, holding the small reeds through which they had been blowing, high above their heads as an offering of gratitude to their God and his hieroglyph, the Sun.

The torn and gashed condition of their sleeping rugs was a small price to pay for their lives, and they sang as they prepared their breakfast, already incorporating the name of their leader, Karne, into a hero's song.

The coming of dawn brought more problems to Gya. Grey faced with weariness he looked helplessly around him, wondering how he could possibly escape notice during the daylight hours.

The palace was so heavily guarded it seemed an impossible task to approach it, and he was beginning to despair of ever helping Isar.

He must find somewhere to hide.

Even as he reached desperation, he found Berka, the ragged child of the night before, staring at him again. She seemed to have an uncanny way of seeing him when he thought he could not be seen.

He stared back at her, unsure whether she was friend or enemy.

He tried smiling to put her at her ease, but the smile was not as relaxed as he had intended it to be.

She did not smile back, but after another prolonged stare she suddenly beckoned to him to follow her. He hesitated. There was still no overt enmity in her eyes, but he could not be certain that there was friendship there either.

He decided to allow his intuition to guide him, and followed her. The fact that she led him from cover to cover and was constantly darting looks, not only at himself, but in every direction, convinced him at last that he was right to trust her. If she were going to give him up to his enemies she would surely have led him straight to them.

They had a few narrow escapes, and each time, it was the presence of mind of the child that saved him. She seemed to be used to this kind of secrecy. She knew the movements of her people, and how to avoid them.

She brought him eventually to a halt, beside a pile of wood and rotting hide, that must once have been a shack. The best timbers had been removed, and rubbish of all sorts had been piled up against the remainder. The smell was sickening, and Gya could not imagine what she intended. He was startled when, with calm assurance, the self-possessed little girl began to move some boards and revealed that the whole heap was hollow inside and would afford adequate shelter.

Obediently he crept past her as she indicated, and she nodded with satisfaction as he took up his cramped position inside.

She pointed at him and mimed sleep.

He nodded, and whispered "thank you," but he was still not sure if she understood his language, he blew her a kiss. This place was bad, but it was better than being captured.

She seemed to understand the kiss and, for a moment, something like unguarded warmth flickered across her wary eyes.

Then she replaced the wood, and was gone.

He was in darkness.

Inside the palace Isar had waited miserably for the dawn, but saw nothing of it when it came.

The small room he was in had no opening, except the one heavily covered with hides and carefully guarded.

The air was stuffy and oppressive, and his one comfort, a small chalk-stone lamp with its flame guttering in a pool of oil, had been removed by the guard not long after he was brought to the palace.

The little chalk-stone lamp had reminded him of his home and he ached to see the smooth, gentle, feminine curves of the chalk-stone hills around the Temple. This was a harsh and rugged land, the hills high and craggy, Na-Groth's plain, a stronghold.

Would he ever see his home again?

He doubted it.

He fell to fitful sleep about the time Gya was being shown to his hiding place by Berka, and Karne's men were celebrating their victory. He did not wake again until he was roughly shaken and dragged out of the room.

He was taken to a larger one where he was pushed on to his knees before the same old man who had originally led him into the palace, the priest of Groth, Gaa-ak.

This time he was too tired, too dazed and too much in pain even to contemplate defiance.

He remained kneeling, looking around him with blood-shot eyes, amazed at the richness and variety of furs that hung upon the walls.

"I trust you are well rested," Gaa-ak said.

Isar looked at him stupidly.

The guard poked at him.

"I slept a little," Isar muttered with a dry throat, thinking of water.

"You are a carver of wood," the old priest of Groth now said, more as a statement than as a question.

Isar showed surprise.

"We knew of your coming," Gaa-ak said in reply to Isar's unspoken question. "We were waiting for you."

"How?"

"We knew."

"I was coming . . ." Isar started to say and then stopped.

"To see Janak, the greatest wood carver this side of the Great Ocean," prompted the harsh voice of Gaa-ak.

Again Isar looked surprised.

"Is he . . . ?"

"He is dead," the old man said coldly.

Isar was shaken. Janak was a great man and there was no one to match him in his skill.

"Na-Groth ordered his death before he knew who he was. A pity. We need him now."

Isar stared at the man.

"We will just have to use you instead," Gaa-ak added coldly.

He was watching the boy closely.

"Did you hear what I said?" He said sharply.

Isar looked at him again, but said nothing.

"We need someone skilled at wood carving. Your life has been spared only because of this."

Isar had wondered why they had not killed him.

He looked around gloomily at the sombre walls, the dark columns.

He had seen no carving in the palace. What did they want carved?

Gaa-ak was pacing up and down, a muscle twitching at the side of his eye, giving him the appearance of a ghoul, winking with a kind of dreadful and deadly bonhomie.

Isar shuddered and looked away.

"Do you not want to know what it is that we must have carved?"

Gaa-ak prodded him with his staff as he said this.

Isar looked at him wearily.

"I want to know," he said obediently, but with no enthusiam.

The priest of Groth looked pleased and conspiratorial.

"Follow me!" he commanded, a gleam of excitement in his eye as he strode from the chamber.

Isar looked questioningly at his guards. They shrugged and hauled him to his feet, keeping a spear at his back as he followed the old man along the dark passages, through the great hall, now empty except for guards, and out through the main door, into the daylight.

Although the sun shone, it was not as it was at Isar's home, flickering through leaves on to the heads of children playing. It was sifted through layers of dirty air to fall dully on dull surfaces.

Isar was marched forward until he stood before the

enormous mass of the Statue of Groth. There he was
pushed roughly to his knees again.

He noticed that many people were on the ground before the Statue, crawling or kneeling, praying in whining, wheedling voices for favours.

The boy who had been used to the Temple of the
Sun looked around him in amazement.

The movement of his head elicited a sharp blow
from Gaa-ak's staff.

"When you are in the presence of Groth you look at
no one but Groth," the old man snapped.

Isar looked at Groth.

Groth had no face.

"Pray. Pray for your life," hissed the old man, giving
him another push with his stick.

Isar prayed. But not to Groth.

"Aloud!" snarled Gaa-ak.

"I do not know the words," stalled Isar feebly.

"Speak after me," the man said, and bowed his stiff
neck reverently to the wood and straw.

Isar felt more sick and more afraid than he had ever
felt before.

"I will not pray to a false god," he thought bitterly.

But if he was to live . . . ?

And if Groth was nothing but wood and straw what
was the harm in it?

Words Kyra had spoken long ago came back to him.

"Thought has power. Belief has power. If people believe in a thing strongly enough they invest it with
power."

He was afraid.

Had this monstrous creation been given power by the people's belief in it?

He heard the old man intoning words in a loud, high pitched, unnatural voice.

"Lord Groth, mightiest god in the universe, hear my plea . . ."

It was clear he expected Isar to repeat them, and when he did not, the guards struck him savagely.

"It is only wood and straw . . . nothing but wood and straw . . ." Isar told himself over and over again, and then, swallowing hard, the pain of the blows bringing sweat to his brow, he said with his mouth the words the priest of Groth wanted to hear, but inside the sanctuary of his own mind he cried to his own God, his own Helpers in the Spirit Realms, his own people.

He shut his eyes and tried with all his might to visualize the Tall Stones of the Temple of his homeland, and the priests who served there. A picture of it came to him, and, instead of the dusty forecourt with the monstrous statue, he saw Kyra and Khu-ren and the priests of the Inner Council walking from Stone to Stone, touching them and intoning the words of the ritual to fend off harm.

Loud and clear he suddenly echoed their words and stood upright, all pain gone, his face transformed.

The old man beside him appeared momentarily to falter and crumple. The supplicants grovelling in the dust at the feet of Groth, looked at him with glazed eyes.

"Spirits of the Realms deeper than man's heart, rise
to our aid.

Spirits of the Realms higher than the Sun, visit us
now at the time of our need."

"Enough!" shrieked the priest of Groth, regaining his
strength. "You are faced with the greatest god the
world has ever known and you blaspheme!"

Isar stood his ground watching impassively as the
old man frothed and ranted.

He knew he would not be killed. They needed him.

Behind him there was a movement and a sound.

Groth's beautiful, cold Queen, with all her entou-
rage, was emerging from the palace. They seemed to
glide across the forecourt with the rhythmic motions of
a snake, and came to rest not far from him.

"What is it you want of me, lady?" Isar said boldly,
meeting her gaze.

She smiled, a small and ominous smile, and her eyes
flicked over him like a whip.

"Has my lord priest not told you?"

"I am to carve something—but what it is I do not
know."

She looked at the old priest.

"He is an old fool and not long for the world," she
said icily.

Isar could see the fear in the old skull face, and felt
almost pity for him.

Behind the Queen he sensed Lark's presence, but
dared not look at her.

"Why," the lady Maeged said, jerking her long robes

about her as she moved imperiously nearer to Isar, "you are to give our god his face. There is no greater honour than that!"

Isar was amazed.

He looked up at Groth's faceless head.

Until now he had felt the vast statue's presence and menace, but had not paid much attention to the details of its construction.

He studied it now with the eye of an artist, and noticed that, apart from its immense size, which was impressive enough, it was built with great skill. Trunks of trees, branches and twigs, were all woven in a way to give it bulk and solidity, the finer details supplied by woven straw.

He wondered why Na-Groth had not seen to the matter of the face before. There was no doubt that the right mask would add much to the image.

Maeged was standing before him, studying him, as he studied Groth.

"You will do it," she said, "or you will die like the man who destroyed the last face."

Isar looked his question, and shivered to see brooding pleasure in the Queen's eyes.

"It was in another country . . . before we came to Klad," she said. "He was killed piece by piece . . . by Groth himself. His face was the last to go."

Isar felt ill and could not resist a quick look at Lark.

In meeting her eyes, he was filled with such strength and comfort, it was almost as though they were free and together again.

He forced himself to look away from her in case the fell Queen intercepted their communication.

"You will do it?" Maeged asked, but the tone of her voice was such that there was no question of his refusal.

"I will do it," he said.

Her eyes flickered like those of a snake darting at its prey.

Swiftly she turned on her heel and snapped her fingers.

Her attendants lifted her trailing robes from the dust and she swept off across the forecourt, back to the palace.

Isar noticed that Lark had taken advantage of the disturbance of the Queen's going, to slip away. The people in the forecourt had fallen upon their faces, the guards were concentrating on Isar, and the old priest. Gaa-ak, was occupied with his own worries.

Isar had the presence of mind to turn away from Lark, so that his following eyes did not give her away. But his heart went with her.

Only Berka, who was watching everything that happened from the shelter of the houses that bordered the place, saw her go and slipped forward to join her.

The Lords of the Sun

The Lord Khu-ren had decided to call together the full power of the Lords of the Sun. This was not lightly nor easily done, but he felt it was justified.

The Great Temple was full of people, men and women alternating, hand in hand, moving rhythmically in circles, the life energy of their bodies helping to increase the power needed for the transfer of Spirit-Forms from across the world.

Within the northern Sanctum the Lord High Priest and the Lady Kyra waited for their peers, feeling the pulse of energy build up around them.

Gradually the beat of the drums and the throbbing of the earth seemed to come from within them.

They felt themselves to be in a vortex where Time and Space and Physical Reality had no meaning. The singing in their heads was the singing of the Spirit

Spheres, the myriad Realms of God, each sphere spinning with its own energy, each humming with its own voice, the full and separate syllables of each sound making up the Secret Name of God, only one letter of which was entrusted to each Sphere, and our whole universe contained, with other universes, in only one of the Spheres.

The name of God was complete.

It had no end, and no beginning.

Kyra was filled with awe at this paradox, and prepared to abandon herself to the vortex.

What she was experiencing now could not be expressed through words available to man. She knew she must let go, let go of the world, of reality as she knew it . . . whatever came she must allow to come, without filtering it through the comforting, but limiting, mesh of her mind.

She could hear the thundering of Presences, feel the pull and tug of light as it spiralled past her, the abrasive wing of darkness as it swooped into the eye of the Vortex.

There was no way back . . . only through . . .

Kyra let go . . .

and in that act of relinquishment so changed the mode of her Being that she burst into the Spirit Sphere in a myriad fragments of Light, each fragment experiencing a form of existence she had never known before.

But the human frame cannot hold such transformations for long, and, trembling with the strain of it, her body in pain from the unusual demands made upon it, she had to return to being Kyra.

Around her in the Inner Sanctum of the Great Temple of the Sun were grouped the Spirit-forms of the Lords of the Sun.

"Is this Reality not enough that I have to take on the knowledge of others?" she thought wearily.

Sometimes the awareness of the immensity of Existence, its complexity and its beauty, was too much to bear.

Sometimes she longed to be an ordinary person, content with the immediate and the visible.

And then she looked around her at the figures of the spirit-travellers from distant places on the earth, and the excitement of knowing that she was part of a growing and limitless process of understanding, filled her with joy.

Khu-ren was communicating their problems to the Lords of the Sun.

They shared, in vision, what he knew of Na-Groth.

One, a tall man in a long feathered cloak, responded with recognition.

He knew of Na-Groth.

Instantly all attention was upon him and Khu-ren's mind was incisive in its questioning.

It seemed that in this particular Lord's country a certain plant grew that was used for making dreams.

In their underground Temple there were bare stone cells where supplicants slept after having inhaled the smoke of the burning plant.

In the morning they would tell the Seer-priest of their dreams and he would interpret them.

Kyra thought about her own priests who had great respect for dreams, but would not have confused illusion with inner reality.

It seemed Na-Groth had been one of these Seer-priests, and, at first, had done his work well and conscientiously. But, as priest, he had free access to the sacred plant and began to use it more and more for his own purposes. At last he claimed that he, and only he, was in touch with God, and God was ordering him to take command of all mankind to lead them to worship him as he had always wanted to be worshipped.

The first indication that the feathered priesthood had that all was not as it should be, was when they began to notice that people were leaving the Temple of the Sacred Smoke tense and worried, instead of relaxed and happy.

Some took their own lives, some the lives of others.

The priests at first were loath to doubt one of their own, but there came a time when Na-Groth's excesses could be ignored no longer.

Their land was in darkness and fear, much as Klad now was.

"You speak of the past. Is your land now free and happy once again?"

"Yes . . . and no. Yes, we defeated Na-Groth. But no, we have not returned to our former innocence, for our people no longer trust the Smoke and our Temple has fallen into disfavour. Our priesthood lives in the hills and is consulted by only a few people. The others prefer to live without a god, than with one they hate. They blame us for Na-Groth's god. You see it is our Sacred Smoke that conjured him to life."

The Lords of the Sun waited patiently for the continuation of the story, their hearts heavy with what they already knew.

It was Kyra who asked the next question.

"How did you defeat Na-Groth?"

The feathered priest looked at her.

"I am ashamed to tell."

"Tell us."

There was a long pause.

Faintly Kyra was aware of the drumming, the pulsing, the turning of the people in the circles beyond their Inner Stone Ring. She knew they could not hold the spirit-travellers for long, the thread was fine and fragile, and time was already straining it.

"We used his mother against him."

The regret in the priest's mind touched all the Lords of the Sun with sorrow.

"How?" prompted Kyra.

"She lived in a village a long way from the temple. Na-Groth had long since abandoned her and she was bent with age and loneliness. We visited her and probed her memory for anything we could find to help us against her son. She was not aware that that was what we were doing."

Again they could feel the pain of his remorse.

"We felt it was justified at the time, but when she found out what we had done, and that it was her words that had helped us to it . . . she killed herself. She still loved her son."

The man's mind was full of grief, and they could all feel the suffering of the mother.

Gently Khu-ren turned their attention from the mother to the son.

"We must know what she told you, and what was done."

His thought was steady and urgent.

"There is not much time!"

"As a young child," the feathered priest continued, "he was savaged in the face by a wild cat, and this has so scarred his memory that he is consumed by the dread of these animals."

The memory of the young Na-Groth's ordeal came to them with terrifying clarity. They lived again the pain as the animal tore at his face. They felt his fear of blindness as he struggled to protect his eyes. They experienced the surge of hate and vengeance that was his as he picked up a stick and flailed at it. When it was felled at last they shared his terrible, cruel joy as he reduced the living creature to a mass of blood and bone and sticky fur.

"We sent our people out with traps and caught two wild cats," the priest of the Sacred Smoke continued, "and then we released them in the temple when Na-Groth was alone.

"I can hear his screams still!"

The great Lords were silent as the tale ended.

But the energy in the Sacred Circle was beginning to dissipate as the weariness of the people circling grew.

Kyra could see the images of those around her beginning to break up and fade.

"We thank you," Khu-ren managed to project. "Perhaps you have helped us to save our land."

The priest of the Temple of Smoke was the last to go.

Khu-ren and Kyra bowed to him.

When he was gone Khu-ren looked at Kyra.

"And so the mother will destroy her son again?" she said regretfully.

"No," Khu-ren said. "The son destroys the son. He was entrusted with a Mystery which he has misused. It is only fitting that fear should destroy the one who rules by fear."

The people of the circles were dispersing, the priests supervising their orderly exit from the Great Temple.

The Inner Council gathered round Khu-ren and Kyra and were told what had taken place.

"How will we use the knowledge?" they asked at once.

But Khu-ren and Kyra were exhausted.

"We will think on it and meet again. This is too important a matter to be decided by tired minds, in haste."

Birds flew down and sat upon the Stones, and in the very place that Kyra had had her experience of the Vortex, a cricket began its familiar song.

The Preparation

Lark looked deep into Berka's eyes and knew that she had found a friend.

Without questioning, she followed the child into the depths of the sprawling, ugly township, Berka's ragged cloak over her shoulders so that she would not be so easily recognized as one of Maeged's slaves.

She was led to the broken wreckage of the house in which Gya lay hidden, and the makeshift entrance door was pulled back.

Inside Gya woke with a jerk from his long and restless sleep, to find himself observed by Berka and a stranger. He was on the defensive at once but the smile of the older girl put him at ease. She put her hand to her lips to indicate that he must make no sound and sat down beside him. Berka remained standing, the cramped conditions not affecting her small frame.

Gently Lark put her hands on Gya's head and shut her eyes.

She seemed to be concentrating deeply.

Puzzled, he stared at her.

So far no words had been used, but he could feel that she was to be trusted.

He found himself thinking about Isar and the adventures they had been through together. Suddenly he had a flash of inspiration. This must be the dumb girl, Lark, Isar had spoken so much about!

As soon as the shock of this registered in his mind, she smiled and opened her eyes, looking straight into his.

"You are Isar's Lark?" he whispered.

She nodded.

He looked shaken.

Berka stood in her customary way, watching and listening.

"Have you seen Isar?" Gya whispered next.

Lark nodded.

"Where?" he almost cried aloud, thinking that if Lark was free, Isar might very well be free too.

Lark could not answer and looked to Berka for help.

"The tall one . . . hair like . . . sun?" the child asked.

Lark nodded.

Berka turned to Gya.

"Groth," she said, haltingly in a language she did not find easy to speak. "He make Groth face."

Gya looked bewildered.

"Groth no face," Berka repeated using her hands to

mime what she was trying to express. She hid her face in her hands and then suddenly revealed it, pulling her features into a fierce and ugly shape. Gya, in spite of the circumstances, could not help laughing.

She pointed to her face as it was now.

"He make. He make," she said.

Gya was still very puzzled, but he decided not to pursue this line of questioning. It now seemed clear Isar was still in the clutches of Na-Groth.

"Will you help me to free him?"

Lark did not know how to mime the answer to this. She wanted to say that she would help him to destroy Groth, and that way he would eventually be free. She wanted to say that it would help neither Isar nor his people if he were taken from the palace now. But she had no tongue to say all this.

She looked at Berka.

The child shrugged. She too did not know how to put into the words of his language the complex thought she had only half caught from the mind of the dumb girl.

It began to dawn on Gya that they were not going to help him.

He gripped Lark's thin wrist roughly.

"You *must* help me!"

He was met with a look of gentle reproach, and he dropped her wrist, ashamed.

But what was to be done?

Now that he was rested he was determined not to stay idle another moment. He would find a way into the palace of skulls and shadows, and out again, without their help!

As he began to gather himself together, the girls could see from his eyes that he was desperate and impatient.

Vigorously Lark shook her head and put a restraining hand upon his arm.

He shook it off angrily.

"You will not help me. I will do what has to be done alone!"

Again she shook her head, her eyes worried.

Berka now took his arm, but he instantly pulled himself free of her small grip.

The two girls looked at each other, and then, together, they looked at Gya.

Their eyes were strange.

It was almost as though they were no longer separate entities, but had become One, and that One was an ancient Being, familiar with the Mysteries.

He drew his breath in sharply as he met the unexpected power in their eyes.

He could not move.

It was as though a voice in his head made it clear to him that he was to follow Berka and that she would show him what he must do.

Isar must be left in the care of Lark.

He bowed his head slightly.

The force with which they held him, left them as suddenly as it had come.

Berka lifted the boards at the entrance and looked out.

"Come!" she said to him in her child's voice.

Still shaken by the experience of what he had seen in the girls' eyes, he followed her.

She led him skilfully between the shacks until Gya became uncomfortable at the distance he was from the palace and his friend. Several times he almost pulled away from her, telling himself he must be crazy to put himself into the hands of a sickly child, an enemy child, but the memory of that special look returned to him, and, although he now began to doubt that it had happened at all, he could not be sure.

She came to a standstill at last before the doorway of a house.

She gave a low call which was immediately answered from within. Gya found himself pushed gently but firmly through the doorway.

Inside he was startled to find himself surrounded by enemies. He clenched his fists and tensed his muscles ready for a fight, but he was not challenged.

Silently the gathering of strangers considered him.

Berka spoke long and persuasively to them in their own tongue and Gya could feel the hostility in their gaze lessening.

When she had stopped speaking, one moved forward and took Gya by the arm to show him he was to sit amongst them.

Gya looked from face to face and everywhere he saw scars, hollow cheeks and haggard eyes. He could almost smell desperation in the air. These people were not the arrogant master race he had seen swaggering about the place, they were hunted animals like Isar himself, though of the same race as the hunters.

Berka had brought him to a meeting of conspirators, dissidents, who were tired of being party to killing and repression, who had finally turned against the laws that took people's loved ones forcibly from them, and forced them to shed their blood in Groth's name.

Many of their number had been discovered and destroyed.

These were the ragged remnants.

They welcomed Gya with reservation. They had been taught to believe the local inhabitants were ignorant savages to be used as a work force, but good for nothing else. They no longer believed this, but it was still not easy to accept one as their equal.

"Berka tells us that you want to join us?"

Gya hesitated, not sure if this was true.

"What is it that you have to offer that would be of use to us?" The slight edge of scorn to the man's voice stung Gya's pride.

"I am a bowman," he said, drawing himself up tall. "Probably the best in the land."

A disbelieving snort came from a man crouching in the shadows.

"Then where is your bow, bowman?" asked the man who had spoken first.

"It was in the possession of a friend when he was captured by Na-Groth's men. It is within the palace."

A murmur went round the group.

"Then it is lost forever!"

"No!" Gya said with conviction.

"Nothing that is taken by Na-Groth is ever free again."

"Na-Groth is a man. He can be outwitted."

There was a tense and uneasy silence in the room.

"Na-Groth is the right hand of Groth. He is no ordinary man."

"Na-Groth is a man like any other man!" insisted Gya.

"He sees everything!"

"He hears everything!"

"He knows everything!"

The voices came whispering out of the shadows and the smell of fear was strong in the room.

Gya suddenly knew why he had been brought here.

He knew what his role was.

These men had been so conditioned to fear Groth and Na-Groth that they were helpless to carry their rebellion through.

They needed a leader from outside the conditioning, outside the fear.

Gya could be that leader.

He knew it, but whether they would follow him was another matter . . .

He stood straight and proud.

"If I prove to you that Na-Groth does not see everything, does not hear everything, does not know everything . . . will you follow me to destroy him?"

Eyes stared at him.

For a long while no one said a word, and then one spoke for all of them.

"If you can prove it," he said, "we will follow you."

Berka smiled with relief and slipped unnoticed from the room and was gone.

Lark had not followed Gya and Berka, but had gone straight back to the Palace.

In her dreams a wise and beautiful old man had come to her and through his eyes she had seen many things.

She knew that he was of the Spirit Realms, but whether he was one of the free Spirits or one of those awaiting rebirth on this earth, she did not yet know. Much would have to happen before she would learn that he was the Spirit form of Maal, the priest-friend of Kyra, Karne and Fern, who had been killed by Wardyke, but who had promised to return when his help was needed.

It was he who had led her to seek for Berka and Gya, and it was he who had given her strength to speak with thoughts and to quell with looks.

On her return to the palace she learned that men had been sent to bring timber for the huge mask that Isar was going to carve.

The place was buzzing with speculation about the Face of Groth.

"It is sacrilege that a local savage is to be given the privilege of carving it!" Lark heard someone say as she passed by.

"No, it is better so," someone else replied. "Whoever carves it cannot live to say he carved the Face of Groth. He will be killed."

"I expect Na-Groth will make a festival of the killing," another voice joined in.

"It will be slow!"

"My woman loves festivals of sacrifice."

"You are lucky. Mine wept for hours after the last one. I had to keep her hidden in case Na-Groth was offended."

"You had better keep her out of sight this time. He does not like people who do not enjoy his festivals."

Lark passed the group and her heart was heavy for Isar.

In her dreams everything had seemed possible.

Now, she was not so sure.

To Deva precious time was passing and the great priests of the Temple of the Sun seemed to be doing nothing to help Isar. She began to wonder if they had any power at all. She began to wonder if Groth was indeed the true god.

"At least he gets results!" thought the girl bitterly.

Kyra had tried to teach her the difference between force and power, between slavery and freedom, but it seemed she had not accepted the lesson.

Groth was holding her love.

It began to seem to her that it was to Groth she should turn for his release.

She searched her mind for all that she had heard about the dark god, and when she had found what she was seeking, she closed her thinking to all else.

Secretly she searched for the little white kid that her

favourite goat had delivered to her at the last full moon. It had been living with her in her chamber until her recent illness, and had been fed with choice scraps from her own food.

She found it in the home of Lea, her mother's friend, the priest of dreams.

From her father's chamber she took the ceremonial knife with the blade of sharp jasper and the wooden handle studded with gold pins. It had never drawn blood, nor was it ever intended that it should. Its function in the Temple rituals was purely symbolic.

Deva hid it now in her tunic and ran with the kid bleating pathetically under her arm, away from the Temple of the Sun to the dark hump of the Haunted Mound that rose so mysterious and high above the low plain to the south west. She had heard that in ancient times it had been used for ceremonies to a strange god and dark ghosts of blood sacrifices were said to haunt the place.

She must not be afraid.

Groth had her lord.

He had the power to release him.

What did her parents know?

Times were changing and a new god was supplanting the old.

She was out of breath when she at last struggled up the steep slope of the Haunted Mound. The animal in her arms, struggling to escape, was much heavier than she had thought it would be, and the knife at her waist seemed to add its strength to drag her down.

But at last she was at the summit and the sun's dark red orb had not yet sunk below the horizon.

"At this moment," she thought, "it is probably touching the head of Groth."

She had started to think of him as associated with the setting of the Sun. The rising of the Sun belonged to the god of her mother.

There was no time to lose.

She gripped the small white animal that she loved, and raised the ritual knife high, fear and guilt singing in her ears to drown the cries for mercy that were welling from deep within herself.

"Groth! Powerful new god of Klad . . . accept the sacrifice of this life I love in return for the life of Isar!"

The animal screamed as she plunged in the knife . . . and screamed again.

It was not dead. The sacrifice was not complete.

Sobbing, she stabbed and stabbed.

The creature screamed and struggled.

Blood was everywhere on its white fur.

Its eyes were full of pain.

They would never leave her.

Sweating and weeping and now screaming herself, she finished the deed at last and stood shuddering over its pathetic little corpse.

The cold shadow of the night crawled across the landscape towards her.

"O God," she sobbed, "what have I done!"

But the God she called was not called Groth.

Karne had a difficult decision to make. He knew he

must take advantage of the confidence his men had gained by the success of their subterfuge, but he was not sure how to do it.

To move deeper into enemy territory without a clear and workable plan was foolhardy. To retreat was unthinkable.

He needed another scheme like the last, something amazing and unexpected.

He walked away from his men and sat upon a flat slab of rock on the top of a hill. From that position his view over the surrounding countryside was wide and clear. Something tugged at his memory but he could not bring it to the surface.

Far below him the trackways that criss-crossed the land looked like the outlines of a pattern. Above him a kestrel hovered a long time and then drifted off on a current of air, to hover again, and this time to plunge and kill.

The two separate images came together in his mind and, in a flash, he found what he had been seeking!

Kyra had travelled in spirit form many years ago to a distant land and had told him how she had found a people there to whom flying was a sacred act, a form of meditation. Karne had been sceptical, but her description had been so detailed and so vivid that by the end he was half-inclined to believe her.

It seemed the fine dry sand of a vast plain was used by the priesthood to hold huge symbolic patterns, which meant nothing when you stood on the ground beside them, but which took shape and meaning if you were far enough above them. To get above them initiates launched themselves from the high cliffs of a mountain range that ran down the west side of the plain, strapped to a frame which held huge sails of thin hide. Instead of crashing to the ground as she would have expected, they drifted out over the plain, slowly and gently, curving to the slightest movements of the air, gazing down upon the sacred markings and drawing strength from them. They came to land a long way from their launching place, unstrapped themselves and walked away unharmed.

"Why not?" Karne ttought. When she had told him of it he had longed to try it out. But the longing and the opportunity had not come together. Now they had, and his determination and his need were going to make it work.

When Gya had said so boldly that he would prove that Na-Groth was fallible, he had no idea how he was going to do it. But his chance came sooner than he expected.

News that one of Na-Groth's armies had been defeated inexplicably by spirits, began to be whispered amongst the inhabitants of the dark plain.

The indiscreet villager who had started the rumour had been instantly put to death as an example to others who might consider undermining Na-Groth's image, and the troop of soldiers who were reputed to be the ones who had fled before the vengeful spirits, were slaughtered as well.

A fresh troop of warriors was despatched at once to the scene of the rumoured battle.

Gya saw his chance.

"We will go with them," he cried. "We will march with the warriors as though we are part of Na-Groth's army. And when we find Isar's people, we will join with them and turn on Na-Groth's troop."

The rebels were doubtful. They had been waiting so long they could not believe the moment to act had really arrived.

"What would we do for weapons?" one asked.

"Did not the troop who were just massacred have weapons?" Gya demanded.

"Yes, but . . ."

"They must be somewhere. Find them!"

He spoke with such authority the men found themselves accepting him as commander without question.

Berka watched with shining eyes, proud of her protégé, and when he shouted "Find them!" she was the first to dart away.

The weapons were found and stolen, the men dressed in the dead warriors' clothes, and ready to march with Gya at the head.

As he raised his arm to start them off Berka returned, out of breath, dirty and badly scratched, but in her hand she carried triumphantly his precious bow and arrows.

In the palace Isar was choosing the wood for the Face of Groth. This was perhaps the most important part of the whole process of carving. The wood must be right. The wood must contain the image. The knife's work was to release it to the vision of others.

Groth's skull-faced servant Gaa-ak had led Isar into
a room much larger and lighter than the one in which
he had been confined. Near the roof were slits where
the spaces between the beams had not been completely
sealed over with reed and hide. Shafts of sunlight
speared the gloom and picked out in grotesque detail
the faces of Groth's servants surrounding him, and the
twisted, gnarled wood they had chosen to bring for
him.

Slowly Isar paced up and down looking at the wood,
Gaa-ak watching impatiently.

"Take your choice!" the old man commanded at
last. "Groth cannot wait forever for his Face."

"Cannot?" questioned Isar, raising his eyebrows.

"Will not!" snapped Gaa-ak.

Isar smiled briefly, but his attention had already left
the man and he was thinking about the wood.

Usually when he was about to make a carving he
stayed alone with the wood for a long time, studying it,
feeling where the image lay and how it could be released. With so many people standing about watching
him, the pressure of time upon his back, the smell of
danger in the air, his inner senses would not function
properly and he could see nothing in the wood waiting
for his blade.

He delayed as long as he could, picking up first one
piece of timber and then the other, running his fingers
over each one in turn.

What was he to do?

On Gaa-ak's nod a guard prodded him painfully
with a spear and he decided he could stall no longer.

He took the first piece of wood that he touched and looked with gloom at it as the other pieces were taken away.

It was a huge, ugly, shapeless piece, with no character and no life.

He felt no urge to create anything out of it.

"Good!" Gaa-ak snapped.

He nodded sharply at one of the guards and the man left the room.

"You will be given your tools, but do not think that as soon as you have a blade in your hand you will be able to escape!"

The old man's eyes glinted dangerously.

"The guards will be doubled and they will all be picked men with instructions to kill."

"But if I am killed. . . ?"

"Groth will have to wait longer for his Face. That is all. It is of no great matter."

Isar was silent and depressed. He felt no joy in taking his carving tools into his hands again, though he had longed for this many times in the past dark days.

Khu-ren and Kyra were on their way to the Temple refreshed and ready to take the next step in their difficult task of defeating Groth, when a disturbance near their home gave them pause. People were shouting and weeping and crowding round something that was carried in the arms of one of them.

The first reaction of the two priests was to continue on their way to the Temple as their work there was urgent, but Kyra's instinct told her that she was needed.

It was her scream that brought Khu-ren swiftly to her side.

The noisy crowd instantly became quiet and drew back, leaving the two great priests kneeling beside the pale, dishevelled figure on the ground. It was Deva, unconscious and covered with dried blood, her face streaked with dust and tears.

Kyra wept for her child, but Khu-ren gently pushed her aside and put his hand on the girl's breast.

"She is alive," he said softly. "Kyra, she is alive."

And then to the silent crowd commandingly:

"What happened? Where did you find her?"

"Beside the Haunted Mound, my lord," the man who had been carrying her said in a low and respectful voice. "She was lying on the ground."

"What is this blood? Where is she wounded?"

Khu-ren searched for the source of the bleeding.

The man who had found her shook his head helplessly.

"I do not know, my lord, I brought her here as quickly as I could."

Khu-ren was puzzled.

There was no wound, but a great deal of blood.

"Fetch the Lord Vann," he commanded, "bring him to our home."

His face was grave.

Several people ran for the healing priest.

Khu-ren prised Kyra loose from her child and lifted the girl in his arms.

"Come," he said, "we will take her home."

Deva walked again in the hot sun of the desert land she had left so long ago. There was the shadow of a horror at the back of her thoughts.

"I will not think of it," she told herself. "I *will* not think of it!"

But although she refused to recognize it, it coloured everything she saw. The garden that had once seemed so beautiful, full of deep green peace, now carried menace in the shadows.

Time had passed in that half-forgotten, former life of hers. She was no longer a child. She was a young woman waiting for news, news on which a life depended.

She paced the white stone paths and stared at the fountains and the lilies which once had seemed so transcendent, but this day she saw nothing but water that was slowing to a trickle and lilies that were dying.

She heard someone approaching and spun round to find her love running towards her, his face distorted with anger and bitterness.

"They are going to execute him!" he cried. "We must rescue him!"

She knew now what the horror was.

She had seen his greatest friend kill the commander of the King's guard in anger.

She had seen the stabbing . . . the blood . . . heard the screams . . .

But what she would never forget were the eyes of the commander at the moment of death!

Deva in her sleeping quarters, Vann and Kyra at her side, tossed her head, her eyes flickering, memories passing through her mind . . . her lover fighting the guard, herself drawing back the bolt of the prison cell, their friend escaping . . . the three of them at sea . . . going to a new land to start a new life . . .

But the dying eyes of the commander followed her there.

And later she saw the same look in the eyes of her love, as he was murdered, and in the eyes of the white kid as she sacrificed him . . . the same blood spilling . . . Would it never end?

She screamed and sat up.

Kyra's anxious face was beside her, her comforting arms around her.

The kindly, grey haired healing priest, Vann, was behind her mother.

She could smell herbs burning in the brazier.

Fully awake now, she looked with wide and frightened eyes around her.

She had killed a living thing, an innocent gentle animal she loved, and she could hear Groth's laughter like thunder over distant mountains.

She looked down at herself. The blood was gone. She had been bathed in sweet smelling water and dressed in fresh robes.

But the questioning eyes of the dying creature were still with her.

Why had she done it?

Kyra stroked her head and the girl pulled away from her.

If her mother only knew . . . ?

"I know," Kyra said gently. "The body of the kid was found."

Deva looked at her aggressively, ready to defend herself.

Kyra looked back at her steadily. There was no accusation in her look, only love.

Deva lowered her face, so that her mother could not see her eyes.

How could she bear it?

"Did Groth hear your prayer?" Kyra now asked quietly.

Deva lifted her chin and her eyes were defiant.

"I do not know," she said. "Did your god hear yours?"

Kyra was silent.

Things had gone further even than she had feared.

Was it now "your god" and "mine," she thought sadly.

Her heart ached.

They were trying to defeat Groth in far away Klad, when he was already stalking in their midst.

Vann held up his hand to prevent her saying anything.

"The child has been through a great deal. She must rest now. Leave us."

Kyra hesitated, but Vann was right.

The expression on the girl's distraught face was enough to show her that the time was not right for teaching or for learning.

Kyra bowed and left the room.

Vann offered Deva a soothing potion.

Her face distorted bitterly as she dashed it from his hand.

"I am not a child," she snapped. "I do not need you. I do not need *any* of you!"

He looked at her long and searchingly and then he too bowed and took his leave.

Alone, Deva flung herself down and sobbed as though she would never stop.

In the palace of Na-Groth, Lark was asleep.

Her sleep was deep and restful at first, and then, slowly, a vision began to form for her.

She tried to ignore it, too tired to accept anything from anyone any more.

But the vision was persistent.

She had to let it come.

Kyra's teacher, the spirit Maal, helped her once again to see what it was necessary for her to see.

She saw the Temple of the Sun, the Tall Stones vibrant with the energy of the priests who stood beside them, Maal pointing to one strange regal figure in feathered cloak. It seemed as though she entered his body and there experienced his memories and his thoughts.

Screaming, she turned to fight off the attack of a

ferocious little animal. She felt fear, agony, saw the malevolence in the creature's eyes!

Terrified, she sprang awake.

And as she looked around the crowded room of sleeping slaves she remembered Na-Groth.

The scar that he had so prominently under his left eye was exactly where she had felt the pain on her face in the dream.

When Karne's men were first told that they were going to construct wings and fly like birds they argued fiercely.

How could this be possible?

It was in the nature of man to walk on the earth and in the nature of birds to fly in the air. To break the laws of nature could lead to nothing but disaster.

"True," Karne said, "but we are not going to break the laws of nature. We are going to use them. A great priestess told me that it can be done, and she will help me now. Trust me. We cannot defeat Groth by ordinary means, we *need* to take him by surprise, to use means unfamiliar to him. Remember the last time?"

They remembered.

They had argued then as well.

Their doubting tongues became still and they worked as Karne commanded them, harder than they ever had before.

Karne would have preferred to have had longer to prepare, better hide available, time to practice the technique—but he knew life had to be taken as it was and not as we would have it.

He was thankful for his curious and questioning nature. When Kyra had first told him about the bird-men he had questioned her about every detail and had drawn from her mind things she had not realized that she had noticed. He had pestered her so much with questions that she had grown impatient, but not before he had formed a very clear picture of how the gliding-frames were constructed.

Now was the time to test her powers of observation, and his own understanding and memory.

A thrill of excited fear passed through his body, but he did not let it show to the men who were now so willingly working for him.

They had found a friendly and courageous village to house them while they worked and many of the villagers insisted on joining in the project, some visiting neighbouring villages to barter and borrow hides from friends.

He knew they did not have much time, so he divided them into two groups, making sure that the one rested while the other worked. He even kept them going through the night, huge fires lit by the villagers to give them light. It was fortunate that this particular village was so tucked behind a hill and forest that it was not easily come upon by Na-Groth's men.

The children were only too happy to keep watch, thoroughly enjoying the bustle and the daring of the situation.

When the first sail-glider was finished, rough and

crude, but possibly ready for flight, the question of testing it arose.

The villagers and Karne's men were gathered at the top of the hill around the strange construction, talking excitedly, when he faced them with the problem.

There was a sudden silence.

They all knew that it had to be done, but it was Karne who had the difficult decision to make.

His wish was to take the risk himself, but he knew that if he were killed his men would turn round and go home. There was no one among them who had shown qualities of leadership necessary for such an unusual and dangerous mission.

Everyone was looking at him, waiting for him to speak.

Slowly he described how he expected the construction to function. He told them the story of the people Kyra had seen. He spoke of movements in the air, pointed to the birds who drifted above them, some of them not even flapping their wings and yet still airborne.

He tried to pass on some of his enthusiasm for experiencing the wonders of flight.

"Look at the birds," he cried, "they go where they will, they are not the slaves of Na-Groth! They fly above him and their droppings fall on his head!"

A nervous gust of laughter passed through the crowd at this, and when it had died down Karne found a young village lad standing before him, his eyes alight with vision.

"Let me, my lord!" he cried. "Let me!"

He was trembling with impatience to try the wings.

Karne looked doubtful.

"No, lad," he said gently, "it is a man's work."

"But I am light," the boy cried, "it will be easier for the wings to lift me."

Karne hesitated.

There was good sense in what the boy said.

"Let him try!" one man cried, anxious to avoid risk to himself.

"Please!" the boy pleaded.

Karne looked around.

"What do your parents say to this?"

The lad turned to his parents and his eyes burned with his longing to be the one to fly like a bird.

Hesitantly the father spoke.

"If it is the only way to defeat Na-Groth . . ."

Karne looked at the boy's mother.

"I do not want him to go," she said, her voice low and full of emotion.

"I do not blame you," Karne said gently. "I am sure it is possible for men to do this thing because my sister has seen it happen, but whether we have built . . ."

Before he could finish the sentence a shout so loud and so horrified went up from the assembled people that Karne spun round . . . in time to see the boy launch himself from the low hill on which they were standing, for a moment hang dizzily in the air and then fall like a stone, his sails of hide buckling as they hit the ground and the struts that had held them wide, splintering.

Screaming, the mother rushed to her son, but Karne reached him first and tore the mess of fabric off him.

"O God! O God!" Words ground from his dry throat. "Let him not be dead! Let him not be dead!"

How could things be undone that were done?

Karne would have given his life at this moment if he could have taken back the boy's courageous, foolish act.

Crowding round him with eyes wide with horror the people saw the frail body bleeding, his flesh torn open to expose his bones.

But he was alive.

Cruelly Karne pushed the hysterical mother aside and set about binding the boy's wounds.

He sent for water, for healing herbs, for rugs to keep his shivering body warm, and then when no more could be done he lifted him in his arms to carry him back to his home.

Walking beside him, his mother and his father were there when he opened his eyes briefly and smiled a rakish, lopsided smile, his mouth half swollen and some of his teeth missing.

"I flew," he whispered triumphantly. "I flew!"

The joy in his voice was unmistakable, though he returned to unconsciousness almost immediately.

Work was stopped on the sail gliders.

Morosely the villagers and Karne's men discussed the accident.

The anxious parents waited beside their son.

Karne walked the night alone, thinking.

The obvious thing would be to abandon the whole idea and think of an alternative.

But Karne could not.

Whether it was his own stubborn interest in the possibility of gliding like a bird ever since he had heard Kyra's description of it, or whether he had some command from the Spirit Realms to go on with it, he could not decide——but he was determined to persist.

The boy's attempt had been premature. There was a skill to the manoeuvring of the thing, quite apart from whether the construction was sound or not. He had jumped without preparation, before Karne could pass on the hints he had learned from Kyra about the essential updraught of air that would give the sails the necessary and initial lift.

He heard the rumble of the men's voices around the evening fires and knew it would not be easy to persuade them to continue with the project.

Gloomily he paced about, worrying about the boy, worring about Isar, worrying about Groth.

At last he sat down, wearily, his back against a small tree, leaning his head until it rested on the bark and he could see up through the branches of feathery leaves to the clear sky and the stars.

Gradually peace began to come to him and he thought he was falling asleep.

But he did not.

He could still see quite clearly all that was around him, the black hump of the hill, the small fires surrounded by dark figures, the glow of light from the house where the crushed boy was struggling for life . . .

But strangely he could no longer hear anything, and the thoughts that had been wrestling in his mind were still.

He held his breath.

He could have sworn he felt the presence of his wife.

Quickly he turned his head, but there was no one there.

And then he recognized the tree against which he was leaning.

It was a Rowan tree—a tree Fern had told him had magical properties, a tree that grew in their garden at home, and which many times he had seen her embracing, heard her talking to.

A Rowan tree.

He turned to it and in the secrecy of darkness clutched it to his breast.

He called to Fern.

He called to Kyra.

He asked for help.

Softly the feathery leaves rustled in the evening breeze.

The tree seemed to sigh.

"Help me," he whispered, "tell me what to do."

The tree did not speak, but as he shut his eyes and laid his forehead on a low branch he felt a sense of great confidence and rest.

Khu-ren stood beside him and told him what healing things to do for the boy.

Kyra stood beside him and told him what to do about the sail gliders.

Joyfully he opened his eyes and although he could see no one, he no longer felt alone.

The night Karne spent with the Rowan tree was spent in a very different way by Na-Groth and his court.

A new supply of the precious plants that gave the Smoke of Dreams had arrived by ship.

Like stone images the guards stood around the hall while the lords and ladies of the palace rolled about in paroxysms of pleasure.

Lark stood beside her mistress and watched her as she lolled from her throne, drooling like a sick old crone, calling in a petulant high-pitched voice for more music and more dancing.

Lark could hear the music and it was the worst she had ever heard. The musicians were afraid for their lives and the instruments they used were harsh sounding compared with those of her own people. They made a kind of scratching, wailing whine which started low and grew higher every moment, the ultimate sound of each rising cadence coinciding with a kind of frenzy in the limbs of those who were under the influence of the Smoke.

The dumb girl looked around and shuddered.

Everyone was pawing everyone else. Clothes were being ripped off and sometimes even flesh, though the victims were so crazed with the effect of the Smoke, they did not even notice that they were bleeding.

She wondered if she could slip away.

The guards were eagle-eyed, but the distractions were many. The smoke from the torches and from the fires in the stone enclosures combined with the fatal Smoke itself to reduce visibility.

She crept as quietly as she could from behind the throne.

A guard made a move to stop her at the doorway, but she held her head high and nodded to the Queen as though to indicate that she had been sent on an errand for her mistress.

He let her pass.

What could such a feeble creature do to endanger the safety of Groth and his Spokesman? She could not even speak, and her arms were as skinny as wren's legs!

Thankfully she broke free of the noise and heat of the orgy.

She slipped down the cold corridors and found her way to where Isar was held, still working by the light of lamps and torches.

Again it was her apparent helplessness that persuaded the bored guards to let her through.

She had found some jars of ale and had brought as many as she could carry. They were accepted with rough humour and a few hearty slaps on the back.

While they were busy with the ale Lark stood beside Isar and looked at his work.

His eyes showed how pleased he was to see her, but he said nothing.

He put down his tools and stood close to her, both of them surveying the block of wood in silence.

She always made him feel peaceful and confident when she was near, though how she could do anything to help him in this harsh place he could not imagine.

He longed to protect *her*, but he did not know how.

The wood was intractable.

He worked at it because if he did not he would be killed, but he still could not feel the image in the wood and had no clear picture of what he was carving.

His instinct was to make a hideous monster face to match what he had learned of the nature of Groth, but he knew that that would be dangerous. Na-Groth and Maeged were expecting something grand and magnificent.

He looked at Lark helplessly.

She was not so thin and ill looking as she had been when they first met. Her shining brown hair was soft and combed to coil around her head, her eyes did not seem so sunken. He noticed for the first time what long lashes she had and how sweetly the curve of her cheek met her chin.

She looked at him with a quick and secret smile as though she had read his thoughts, and he flushed slightly.

What was he doing?

Deva was his love and Deva would be his love forever.

Lark moved away from him as though she had caught that thought as well.

With her slender back to him she rested her hands on the wood.

She seemed to be stroking it with her long and sensitive fingers.

Isar stepped sideways so that he could see what she was doing, but there was nothing to see except a girl touching dead wood.

When she was gone he picked up his blade and looked at the wood again.

Suddenly he could see the image in the wood that he must carve as clearly as though it were already there.

He gasped and looked at the guards to see if they had noticed the transformation.

But it was clear that no change was visible to them.

However it had come about, Isar now knew exactly what he must do, and from then on worked with an eagerness and a dedication that surprised the men who were closeted with him.

The same eagerness and dedication were present in Karne's heart as he struggled by himself to perfect the second of the sail gliders.

No one would help him and indeed, he asked no one, but he was determined to show them that it could be done.

The boy was amazingly much better after the treatment Karne gave him, but it would be a long time, if ever, that he walked again.

The villagers had become sullen and unco-operative, and his own men listless and depressed. They were murmuring again about retreat, but Karne managed to persuade them to wait for one more trial, and this time, he promised, he would test it himself.

In spite of themselves the men were curious and, although they would not help, they did not hinder him.

At last it was ready to Karne's satisfaction and the whole population gathered round the small steep hill to watch what would happen.

Gerd, the boy who had made the first attempt, insisted on being carried to a place where he could see. His own suffering had not lessened his enthusiasm for flying like a bird, and he was determined to share the experience of the others in any way that was possible.

His mother did not try to stop him. She respected his need to know. The ways of the living Spirit were mysterious, and she was not one to believe that our flesh and bones are all that we have.

She sat beside him and propped him up against a tree trunk so that he could see what Karne was doing. She was undecided whether the man was mad or inspired by Spirits, but at least now it was his own life he was risking.

Standing at the top of the hill at the edge of a low cliff, with the faces of so many doubting people turned up to him and the heavy harness of the sails chafing at his body, Karne felt sick with fear and realized just how brave the boy must have been to launch himself into the air.

Above him a bird wheeled slowly and gracefully. Karne watched it, remembering Kyra had spoken of the use of unseen movements in the air. The bird was using them. He would use them too.

He looked down to the village and the green sward beside the Rowan tree where he had felt the presence of those he loved.

He called one of his men to fetch him a twig of the Rowan tree. Had not Fern said its magic properties extended to protecting one from harm? He would not like to make the leap without a talisman.

The people waited patiently as the man ran for the twig.

They understood, and quietly touched the things about their own bodies that they used for talismans, pebbles with holes threaded as pendants, rings and bracelets, and one comb of walrus ivory a sailor had brought home from cold and distant seas.

Karne took the twig and lashed it to the cross-beam of his frail craft.

It gave him comfort and confidence.

Everyone was silent as Karne, the Spear-lord, looked once more at the sky and then, giving a wild, strange cry which was at once a prayer and a release of tension, leapt into the space that had so cruelly treated the boy Gerd.

Silently they watched, scarcely breathing, as he was taken up by the draught and then, gracefully, slowly, began to slide down the invisible slopes of the air currents, his flight curving as he turned the bar of wood in

his hand, landing with nothing more than a jolt on the
grass behind the hill.

Then there was no more silence.

Every throat was opened in joyous sound.

They had witnessed what no man among them had
thought possible.

With one tremendous sound the people's voice rose
higher than the highest bird.

Gerd's mother hugged her son, her own eyes so full
of tears, she did not notice that his were the same.

"But I was the first," he whispered. "I was the first!
No one can take that away from me."

They were left alone as the crowd rushed to congrat-
ulate Karne.

What damage he had escaped in the landing he almost sustained during the congratulations. Everyone
was pounding on his back, tugging at his arms, kissing
him, shaking him.

Laughing, he broke away at last.

"Wait, wait!" he cried, "you will break the wings.
Stand back. Stand back."

He managed to pull the sail glider clear and somehow break away from his admirers.

"Tonight we will feast," he shouted, and the shout
of their delight rang in his ears. "But," he added, "tomorrow we will go back to work, and we will work
harder and faster than we have worked before!"

They laughed and groaned. He drove them hard, but
who would not be proud to work for such a hero?

They danced and sang late into the night, but Karne insisted that the hero song should be given to the boy Gerd.

"He was the first," he said. 'He was the bravest one of all. The song must be of him and it will be sung when all who are here now have long since gone beneath the burial mounds. We will carry it to the Great Temple of the Sun and it will be sung on the days of festival and rejoicing!"

The people cheered.

The people sang.

The boy hardly noticed the throbbing and the pain as the words of praise rang around him.

His eyes shone.

The Face of Groth

While Na-Groth's soldiers marched, they sang. They had no doubt that they were stronger than the enemy and would soon be marching triumphantly back to their lord and his queen, leaving a tasty feast for the scavenger birds and beasts.

What they did not know was that Karne was preparing a surprise for them, and that the other troop that marched so smartly with them and sang louder than any of them, was itself the enemy.

Spies brought reports of enemy sighted in a particularly hilly area. Numbers were not known, but it seemed clear that a village was being used as the meeting place for the groups of fighting men that were gradually gathering from the east.

"The village must be punished as an example to other villages," the Captain said with determination.

"Not a living person must escape the wrath of Groth. The fighting men we will kill in battle. The villagers, all but one, we will tie to stakes and set alight. The one we have spared will take our message to the other communities. No one will dare to help these circle stammerers, these maudlin mumblers again!"

Gya could feel rage spreading hotly through his body and his knuckles were white as he gripped his bow.

Circle stammerers! Maudlin mumblers!

So that was how these grunting hogs saw the ancient and splendid ritual of his people. He would show them!

He would show them the power of the Circle! The energy of prayer!

He leapt up and raised his bow, his mind on fire with rage. Deadly as a hawk's eye on a field mouse, he aimed his shaft momentarily at the heart of the very man who had spoken these words.

The whole scene froze. Every eye was upon him.

Not a sound or movement broke the tension.

The Captain's eyes glazed with sudden fear, but his men scarcely grasped what was happening.

In another moment he would have been dead and probably Gya and all his small troop of dissidents as well, the possibility of Karne's victory lost, the Sun Temple civilization destroyed.

On Gya's arrow all this hung.

Like a wave the moment paused at the point of breaking.

Inside his head a voice was screaming:

"Kill!"

But from the trees, from the sky, from the rocks and grass and bracken . . . voices were pleading with him to hold . . . this was no way to prove his God.

Sweating, he raised his arm higher, and shot into the sky.

Clean and true his arrow sang and flew, sucking with it the breath of all who watched.

"Destruction to the enemy!" shouted Gya.

"Death!" the men around him roared, and where there had been silence, spears on shields were banged to make as much noise as possible.

Only the Captain was silent, pale and shaken and sweating from his experience.

His eyes were full of hate and menace as he met those of Gya.

When the next dawn came and Na-Groth's men advanced to attack the village, Gya and his troop made sure they were well behind the main attacking body.

The Captain expected an easy victory, but Na-Groth was not the only one with spies.

Karne was well aware of the forces advancing against him.

As Na-Groth's army crept nearer the apparently sleeping village through the damp and dewy grass, the early morning mist lying close to the ground reducing visibility for either side, they had no thought that this might be their last engagement in Na-Groth's service.

When the Captain judged that they were near enough he gave a low whistle and stood up, his arm in its black leather arm-guard, signalling his men on.

Swiftly they moved now, flattening the nettles and the tall grasses, spears at throwing readiness, sword hilts gripped tightly.

Behind them Gya's men crouched and waited.

In front of them and from the east the huge sphere of the sun began to rise behind the highest hill, and, as it it came almost to full splendour, the soldiers looked up at it and were aghast to see silhouetted blackly against its burning copper, huge bird shapes like nothing they had seen before.

Even as they stared the air became full of strange wailing, whining noises, eerie as ghosts, loud as horns.

The shapes moved forward.

The shapes began to fly.

Dazzled by the sun the men of Na-Groth were faced with huge black wings that spread above them menacingly and hung in the air as though waiting to pounce upon their prey.

Screaming, they turned and ran.

Gya's men were waiting for them.

Too far back to see the strange birds, Gya could not understand what had put the warriors to flight, but he knew that he must not let them return to Na-Groth to be used again in greater strength against his friends.

His bow sang out.

The axes, spears and swords of his friends were put to work.

Astonished, Karne saw the soldiers of his enemy turn upon each other and do battle.

He landed the lead glider safely and called to his men to follow him.

Exuberant at the success of their plan they followed him gladly.

Caught between two enemies, Na-Groth's men had very little chance.

The fighting was fierce and many were killed. Those that were not, were taken prisoner and shown a mercy that surprised them.

Gya was brought to Karne.

"This man fought on our side, my lord," he was told.

Karne looked into the young man's eyes and saw honour there.

"You are not of Na-Groth's people?" Karne asked.

"No, my Lord, but these who fought so bravely with me are. I would ask you to set them free."

"How is it that they fight against their own?"

"They have no love for Na-Groth, lord, and would join with us in overthrowing him."

"Good news indeed. Are there more that we may count upon?"

"I do not know for sure, but it is possible. There is much dissatisfaction and despair."

"Fear too, I think."

"Yes. Fear too."

Karne looked at Gya steadily.

"You do not fear?"

"Not enough it seems," Gya answered cryptically, with a smile.

Karne smiled too and clasped his arm in friendship, right over right, as was the custom.

"You are the Spear-lord Karne?" Gya now asked.

The older man was surprised his name was known, but when he heard that Gya was a friend of Isar's and had news of him tears of joy and relief came to his eyes.

But they were short lived. Isar was still a prisoner and in danger. This day's work had only defeated a small part of Na-Groth's force.

"It is important no news of this battle should reach Na-Groth's ears," Karne told his men. "Not one of these," and here he indicated the prisoners, "must be allowed to escape. We must move deeper into Na-Groths territory and finish what we have started. It will not be easy and each one of you has to give up thought of personal peace and comfort until Na-Groth is defeated." He looked searchingly into the eyes of his followers.

"Is that understood?"

"Aye," they murmured.

"Are you with me?" he called ringingly.

"Aye!" they replied, this time loudly and convincingly.

"Good," he said shortly, and then he turned to Gya.

"You know the country. You know the stronghold of Na-Groth. Lead us."

As they moved away, leaving the villagers to handle the prisoners, the wounded and the burials, Gya met the eyes of the defeated Captain.

If ever eyes could bore into the soul of another and bring a curse, those eyes would have done it then.

Having seen what happened at the hands of Na-Groth to the first troop of men who had been defeated by Karne's tricks, the second troop were not at all keen to escape and return to their master. They made willing, if ungracious prisoners.

All except one.

The Captain had a score to settle with Gya and within half a day of Karne's departure for Na-Groth's stronghold, he managed to elude his captors and disappear.

As soon as they discovered he was missing the villagers sent the older children out to look for him, but he had already covered too much ground and was out of reach.

Gerd, lying impatiently on his bed of straw and rugs, fuming with frustration, could not help thinking that he would have been able to track him down if only he had been able to walk.

Now what would become of Karne?

But Karne himself was making good progress and was full of confidence.

The men who were moving the seven sail gliders worked their way across country more or less under cover, but the main force, dressed in the clothing stolen from Na-Groth's defeated men, marched boldly forward. When talking had to be done Gya's dissidents did it so that the difference in language would not be noticed.

They even managed to send a false message to Na-Groth that the Temple forces had been routed.

This way they hoped to make him relax his vigilence.

What they did not know however, was that the Captain of Na-Groth's defeated troop was making his way back to his master at the same time, but by a different route.

To Gaa-ak kneeling at the feet of Groth at the dawning of the day that was to be the Festival of the Mask, the sky appeared to be on fire. From east to west clouds flaming with the red anger of the sun mottled the sky, forming a low and menacing roof.

As Gaa-ak mouthed the prayers the people expected of him, his eyes were drawn involuntarily upwards several times.

What did it mean?

He had lived long in Na-Groth's employ, but had never seen a sky quite so strange and so lurid.

Through the mottling of fire the distant universe showed, a potent and a vibrant blue. Momentarily the priest of Groth had a chilling premonition of danger.

At dawn he always felt vulnerable.

Groth's time was sunset, the moment of his triumphal entry into the Dark Kingdom where he

chastised those who had offended him and rewarded
those who supported him.

The day was the sun's time and Groth's influence
was at its weakest.

During the day he bided his time.

During the night he came into his own.

The ceremony of dedication at which the Mask was
to be offered to the god would take place at noon, the
moment of balance between the two powers, the moment of increase for Groth.

Gaa-ak's task at dawn was to start the prayers and
incantations and continue them until at noon the whole
population was gathered to do obeisance to the powerful lord.

By sunset the god would be used to his new Face
and would wear it proudly into the night.

Na-Groth and Maeged would not join their people
until the Mask was carried out in procession ready for
the final ceremony.

Na-Groth was sleeping late.

It was Maeged who swept into the room where Isar
was smoothing the last surface on his masterpiece.

She walked around the giant mask, in itself just tall-
er than a man, and stared at it with baleful intensity.

It was powerful, there was no doubt.

The boy who looked so feeble had great strength of
vision and skill in translating it to wood.

"But there is something of the animal in this face,"
she said suspiciously.

Behind her, Lark met his eyes and he was given confidence to answer boldly.

"Is Groth not master of animal and man? Is Groth not master of all things?"

Luckily she did not detect the sarcasm in his voice.

"True," she said doubtfully, not quite sure what it was about the mask that disquieted her.

Thoughtfully she prowled about it, looking at it from every angle, but it was more man than animal, and more god than man, so she retired at last, content to let it be.

It was certainly better than the last one that Groth had had.

And what if it was not perfect, what did it matter?

NaGroth had just wanted an excuse for a sacrificial ceremony. He enjoyed the drama of other people's suffering and death as she enjoyed power and adulation.

To her and her husband Groth was wood and straw.

They were the real gods, the dispensers of life and death.

They despised the people who crawled about the base of the Image they had created.

Deva was withdrawing more and more from her family and friends.

She refused to attend any prayer rituals in the Sacred Circle of the Temple and slipped away as often as she could to the Haunted Mound, secretly saying her prayers to Groth, using the height of the Mound to see as far as she could towards the west where Isar was, and where Groth's fell kingdom was.

Her parents were busy almost continually in the Temple now and she saw her mother only when she came home to rest, grey with weariness.

Several times Kyra tried to talk to her daughter, seeing her sullen and brooding face, but each time Deva managed to repulse her, and at last, too tired to fight any more, Kyra left the girl, thinking that the greatest service she could do for her would be to defeat Groth and bring Isar home to her.

"As soon as we have something positive to tell her she will come round," Kyra told herself.

Although she loved Deva deeply, she knew, compared to Khu-ren and herself, and indeed to Isar, she had not evolved through so many lives, nor reached so fine an understanding of life's mysteries.

On the day of the Festival of Groth's Mask Deva rose early and was drawn to the Mound.

Looking at the strangely lurid mottling of the sky she felt that this was somehow a day marked out for dramatic events.

"Today I will free my lord," she said to herself, "and if I do not, today he and I will die."

She felt no fear.

She said it calmly, knowing that if Isar died she would join him.

Inside the folds of her cloak she carried the same knife she had used when she had made her first sacrifice to Groth.

In the Temple of the Sun the strange and beautiful appearance of the sky was also seen as an omen.

There was a calmness and a readiness in the hearts of the priests that had not been there before.

This was an important day and on this day they would put all the energy that they were capable of into the challenge of Groth.

Karne took the appearance of the sky as a promise from the God of Light.

"See," he declared to his uneasy troops, "it is the light of sunrise, of renewal . . . this day will be a good day!"

Gya had shown them where to make camp the night before, so that at the dawn they would not be far from the ridge of hills that rimmed and protected Na-Groth's stronghold.

They had planned their attack well and had every justification for expecting success.

But Na-Groth's defeated Captain had reached the ridge before them and was at this very moment warning the guard of their approach.

Exhausted he lay down to recover while they prepared their defences.

He would have liked to deliver the message immediately to Na-Groth and receive the reward he was sure would be his due, but his limbs were aching with the strain of the speed with which he had covered the ground from the rebel village, and his heart was longing to avenge himself on Gya.

The sweetness of reward could wait.

Karne moved his men carefully closer to the pass and then called a halt.

Puzzled, Gya came to him.

"We must move forward now," he said, "we are too near to remain unnoticed for long."

"I know," Karne said, a slight frown of concentration between his eyes. "But I need to think."

"Think!" hissed Gya in amazement. "Surely we have done enough of that?"

"Something is holding me back," Karne said stubbornly.

"Fear?" the young bowman asked bitterly.

He was chafing to get going and was astonished that Karne, who had seemed so impatient himself a few moments before, was now so content to wait.

"No, not fear. Caution perhaps."

"But caution tells us to *move*—before it is too late!"

"Something . . ." worried Karne.

He could not explain it, but he just *felt* it was not the time to move forward.

Even as the two men stood confronting each other, Gya's eyes blazing with accusation and Karne's sombre with the weight of decision, the ominous, rumbling sound of many men marching came to them.

Instantly Karne gave the signal to take cover and lie low.

Not far from their hiding place, but mercifully unaware of them, a large body of Na-Groth's warriors marched towards the pass.

Gya looked at Karne.

If they had been on the move as he had tried to insist, they would have been in the open now, out-numbered, surprised and certainly massacred.

"Na-Groth's special men," one of the dissidents whispered. "No one passes them!"

Karne shivered slightly and said a quiet prayer of thanks to whoever it was who had made him hesitate.

"What do we do now?" someone asked.

"We wait until they are well past the guards and down the other side," Karne said.

They waited.

Gradually the violent red of the sky faded and the canopy of broken cloud that had been so bright before, became dull and slate grey.

The waiting was not easy, and hearts that had been full of purpose and courage began to be afraid.

They watched the strong and disciplined body of men march up the path to the pass. If these were the kind of men that they would have to do battle with, Karne's inexperienced farmers were not at all sure that they wanted to go on.

The dissidents were desperate men and had no way to go but forward, and Gya was anxious to avenge his father and rescue his friend, but Karne could see the hesitation in his own men's eyes.

He was just drawing breath to make an encouraging speech when someone shouted "Look!"

They all looked.

And what they saw astonished them.

No sooner was Na-Groth's special troop at the top

of the pass than Na-Groth's guards let fly spears and arrows at them.

Caught by surprise, the men stumbled helplessly about, attacked on all sides by their own people.

Those that survived the first onslaught and recovered their wits fought fiercely back.

Before the startled eyes of Karne's troop a bloody and vicious battle raged without their having to risk a man.

"What is happening?" they gasped.

They could not know that the escaped Captain had brought a message to the guards that a troop of enemy disguised as Na-Groth's men was approaching the Pass and must be stopped at all costs.

Too late the Captain realized the mistake they had made and leapt out to call for a halt to the slaughter.

An arrow from one of Na-Groth's bowmen hit him in the face and he died before the words could leave his mouth.

"Now!" shouted Karne. "Now is the time to move."

And they moved . . . swiftly and neatly and full of courage.

What exactly was happening they did not know, but it seemed clear that the advantage was on their side.

They reached the pass unnoticed and with ease took those who were left alive.

Under the leaden lid of the sky the prayers to Groth were mounting feverishly.

Stamping in the dusty earth a host of dancers clad in animal skins and wearing fearful masks, was causing a red haze to rise around his mighty legs.

Innumerable drummers brought thunder to the air, while the high-pitched wail of a goatskin and pipe threaded a note of hysteria through the crowd.

Everyone on the plain was gathered around the feet of Groth.

Everyone was doing obeisance, sobbing and wailing.

Na-Groth himself, and his queen, were silent, mounted on raised wooden thrones before him, watching with gloating intensity as priests climbed dangerously on the immense body, dragging the mask on long hide ropes to its position over the blank face.

Isar was on his knees, bound, before the throne of Na-Groth.

He too was silent, though the pain of his bindings almost made him cry out, and the fear of the torturous death that he knew he was to suffer at the high point of the ceremony, made his stomach hurt.

He tried to ignore the wild and demonic sounds of the mob around him, tried to go into the Silence Kyra and Fern used so often for comfort and renewal, but the fear and the pain were too strong. He regretted that he had not trained himself as they had trained themselves, making a habit of meditation and quiet. He had been content to enter the Silence only while he was absorbed in carving, forgetting that under such peaceful circumstances, to slip from one level of awareness to another was easy and natural, and required no skill.

The Mask was finally lashed in place just before noon, but not before one of the priests had lost his footing on the massive shoulders of the god and had fallen, screaming, to his death at the feet of Na-Groth. A momentary shocked silence had come upon the people then. Na-Groth filled it with his voice.

"All who climb upon the god will die. No man can live who has profaned the god!"

The priests who were fixing the Mask went cold at this, but the crowd roared its approval, and the dancing and the drumming started up again.

There were those who did not enjoy Groth's ways, but were afraid to be seen to dissent. They shouted louder than the rest, and stamped with greater fury.

Gaa-ak looked up at the sun.

He knew the point it must reach before it began its long slow slide to evening.

He raised his arms and all Groth's priests took their places for the Noon Ceremony.

He did not notice that Na-Groth had half risen from his seat and was staring at the Mask of Groth with fascinated horror.

"What is it, my lord?" whispered Maeged urgently, the only one to notice the expression on her husband's face.

He did not reply.

His eyes did not leave the Face of Groth.

Gaa-ak gave the final signal and all noise and movement instantly ceased.

All eyes turned to the Mask of Groth.

Painfully Isar raised his eyes with the rest and gazed bitterly at his handiwork.

Had he been born for this, to give strength to a curel and wrathful deity and destroy his own people?

If they would only kill him he would gladly die.

He should have killed himself before he used his skill for such a purpose.

No one noticed a small, thin girl and a tall, slender boy slip into position. She was carrying a bundle of marsh reeds dipped in fat and set on fire. He was carrying a finely made bow and a quiver full of arrows, bound with cloth and dipped in oil.

"Now!" Berka whispered.

He fitted an arrow, touched it to the flame of her torch, drew back the bowstring, his eye gazing with deadly accuracy into the dark depths of the eye of Groth.

Silent were the people at the feet of Groth.

Silent the monstrous god.

But through that silence came the whine of a single arrow flying to its mark.

"Ai-i-i . . ." wailed the crowd as the flaming arrow passed dead centre through the eye of Groth and the straw that was packed behind the Mask caught fire.

Within moments the face of Groth was transformed.

Fire leapt from his eyes and through his open mouth.

The people cringed and howled, falling back upon those behind them and crushing many in their haste to get away from the god who had become too terrifying to look upon.

But there were many who turned to Na-Groth for comfort in this moment of horror, only to find that he was screaming and cringing like themselves, his arms covering his face, his voice high pitched like a child's.

"Take it away! Kill it!" he shrieked, beating wth his arms as though it were attacking him.

The dreadful memory of the wild cat lived again in the blazing animal face of Groth.

"Destroy it!" he roared at his horrified priests and soldiers, pointing a shaking finger at Groth.

"Destroy it . . . ! I command it . . . ! Death to the man who does not do my bidding!"

The sound of the crowd changed, the mood turned, the fear they had felt for Groth was released in hate.

"Destroy!" they screamed and charged the sagging god.

As the flames gained power the whole figure began to disintegrate, the onslaught of the people accelerating the process.

The face that had seemed so fearful at first began to appear ludicrous as it was half consumed by fire.

There was an expression almost of bewilderment for a moment.

Some of those who were throwing the rocks paused to laugh.

Had they been afraid of *this*?

The thrones of Na-Groth and Maeged were over-turned as the hysterical crowd surged forward, but the two managed to jump free, Maeged pulling at the arm of her distraught lord, his face bleeding from the scratches of his own nails as he tried to pull the imaginary animal from his flesh, his eyes crazed with fear.

But even as the people thought they were clear of Groth a new menace appeared to threaten them.

In the sky, gliding like giant bats, seven Beings were hovering over them.

Their shadows made the people look up and, as Groth finally fell to earth in a shower of sparks, the crowd gasped at what they saw.

On the ridge beyond the plain a strange and beautiful light, centered in two shining Beings, broke the gloom and darkness of the sky.

Above them the winged shadows hovered.

Behind them the fire of their god's destruction roared, and beyond and around them every house in the plain was a plume of black smoke.

Karne's warriors had set the whole encampment on fire.

With nowhere to turn the people fell upon their faces.

Na-Groth turned on his wife and gripped her throat. In his crazed mind, because she was plucking at him, he associated her with the animal he feared, the animal who yet again was causing his downfall.

"Die!" he screamed.

And together they fell to death as the spear of one of his own men pierced his heart.

When the crowd had charged Isar would certainly have been killed had Lark not swiftly pulled him aside, and then, with the help of Berka and Gya, removed him to a safe place where they unbound and hugged him.

The four of them were scarcely aware of what was happening on the plain they were so happy to be with each other.

"What on earth?" gasped Isar at last.

Gya laughed and shook his head.

"The world has gone mad!"

Isar looked up and stared open mouthed at the sail gliders that were now coming in to land, the people scattering before them like chaff before the wind.

"Those are your father's creations," Gya said to Isar. "He is a great man."

"Karne?" cried Isar, finding it difficult to understand all that was happening.

"Yes, Karne. He built the sails for flying. He led us here. He is a great leader and a great hero."

Gya's eyes shone with admiration.

Tears were in Isar's eyes and he was struggling to his feet, Lark's arms around him to help him up.

"Where is he?"

"He will be with the sails," said Gya. "Come," and he put his arm under the other arm of Isar and he and Lark helped him towards the place where the sail birds had landed.

When Karne saw him he squeezed him so close to his heart with joy and relief that Isar had to cry out for mercy. There were many places on his body that hurt from the beatings and the tortures he had endured.

Karne held him at arm's length and saw how the boy had been treated. Tears of pity came to his eyes.

"I am all right," Isar said, seeing his look. "Everything is all right now."

One of Karne's men began to tug at Karne's arm.

"My lord," he said urgently, "you must come. The crowd is restless and uneasy. You must speak to them."

Quickly Karne took command again and with a few brief orders caused a platform of unburnt wood to be raised.

His sail gliders were arranged in such a way around the platform that they formed a kind of winged sanctuary, out of which he appeared to rise.

He raised his hand and, meekly, those who had survived the recent disorders gathered before him.

Leaderless, they were very different from the people who had terrorized the land of Klad.

The first order he gave was for the burning of the Palace of Skulls.

The next was for the election of a Council of Elders to rule in Na-Groth's place.

He was about to raise his arm again when the two shining Beings who had loomed so hugely on the ridge of hills appeared on either side of him.

The vibrations of fear and hate that had kept Khuren and Kyra out during Na-Groth's reign were now much weaker. The two Lords of the Sun were free at last to enter the place.

Everyone gasped and gazed and fell at their feet.

"Rise up," Kyra said. "No man should crawl before another."

"But you are gods!"

"No," Khu-ren said. "We are priests of the Temple of the Sun, beings like yourselves."

"Tell us who your god is and we will worship him!"

"Our God is not like Groth. You cannot decide to worship him one day and destroy him the next."

"Tell us where he is!" someone cried. "We will follow him!"

Khu-ren and Kyra looked at each other and smiled.

"The beginning is within yourselves," they said. "No further than that."

Bewildered the people stared at the two bright strangers, and even as they stared the air on either side of Karne began to shimmer, the images to break up.

The Lords of the Sun were gone.

All eyes turned to Karne.

He spoke boldly and firmly.

"All those who want to stay in our country must learn our ways and live as we do.

"Those who do not wish to, are free to go, but they must go now.

"We have no time for recriminations, for revenge and misery.

"There is too much to do, and too much to undo."

The Lifting of the Shadow

When Kyra returned to her body she was quick to look for Deva, in spite of great weariness.

When she could find her nowhere near her home, or the Temple, she was filled with alarm and went straight to the Haunted Mound, remembering that it was there that Deva had sacrificed to Groth, and that she had "lived" as a shade for so long before her present incarnation.

She found the girl unconscious once again, the ceremonial knife beside her, bleeding from both wrists.

Her face as pale as her daughter's, Kyra tore strips from her own gown and bound the arms so that the bleeding would stop.

"O child, when will you learn?" she wept, and gathered the limp body in her arms.

Khu-ren, informed by Lea of Kyra's whereabouts,

found them there and carried Deva home, Kyra trailing
behind, sick with unhappiness in spite of the great joy
she should have been feeling for the victory they had
just won.

The Temple community knew of no such unhappiness.

Everywhere was dancing and singing.

Feasting was being prepared and a special ceremony
of thanksgiving.

Everyone seemed on the move, talking and laughing.

Garlands were strung from house to house.

Children were running about underfoot and no one
was chiding them.

This was a great day for the people of the Sacred
Stones and it would be long remembered.

Unwilling to put a shadow over their happiness, Khu-
ren and Kyra slipped through back ways to their home,
and drew the door hangings tightly.

Only Vann and Lea were summoned, old friends
and skilful priests. They worked long and hard on
Deva and at last managed to encourage a flicker of life
in her.

Her wounds were bound with healing leaves, a be-
neficial potion made from other herbs, held to her
white lips.

"Drink my love," Kyra whispered, holding the girl
propped up in her arms, Vann gently pressing the cup
to her lip.

Deva's eyes opened.

Vann looked into them and they were dark and fathomless wells.

She showed no sign of recognizing him.

"You are gracious, my lord," she whispered as faintly as a summer breeze through grass, "to take me in the place of the lord Isar."

Vann looked at Kyra quickly, a question in his eyes.

Kyra looked at puzzled and held her daughter closer.

"Deva," she said gently. "You are safe. You are at home with those you love and Isar is alive and will soon be here."

"I know," murmured the girl dreamily. "My lord Groth has given Isar life. He has taken me instead. I shall live at his court and be his queen."

"No, Deva no! Groth is destroyed. Groth never was a god."

"You will be punished, lady, for such blasphemy!" Deva's voice grew stronger and she looked at Kyra with a hard dark look.

"No one will be punished any more," Kyra said sharply. "Those days are over. We are taught, we learn, we experience the results of our actions . . . we are not *punished*!"

"Those are the ways of the old god, Mother. You will have to learn the new ways or you will not be allowed to visit me at court."

"Deva!" sighed Kyra, her heart close to breaking.

But there seemed to be no way through to her.

Karne stayed on in Kald to supervise the beginning of the new era, Gya his right hand man.

Isar was sent home with those of Karne's men who could be spared. Lark was to travel part of the way with him, leaving him when she reached her own village.

Berka and her family joined with them too, seeking a new home, the associations of Na-Groth's plain being too unpleasant for them.

The news of Na-Groth's defeat spread like fire before a wind throughout a dry country.

Most of Na-Groth's men who were left cut off in isolated places fled towards the coast, hoping to find trading ships to take them far away, but some surrendered to the local communities and asked for pardon.

Some villages were merciful.

Some were not.

Gerd's village sent people to welcome Isar and his group with pipes and lutes, and danced them back to the village.

There they found the Rowan tree had been decked with flowers from all the fields and hills around and was the centre of the celebration. Round and round the people danced and sang, certain that its magic properties had had something to do with the success of the whole expedition.

Isar asked at once to meet Gerd and found him seated on a special carrying chair that had been constructed for him out of young willow wands. The boy's eyes shone to hear the tale that Isar had to tell, and Isar in his turn was sung the song of Gerd's first flight.

As soon as Gerd's mother saw Berka's pale, pinched face and festering sores, she took her in hand and mixed her up special concoctions of herbs. She insisted that Berka and her family should stay with them awhile.

How different this green and feritle village was from the over-crowded plain Berka had known before. Here there was air and light, white water falling from a hill and trees growing in lovely profusion everywhere.

"Let us stay here forever!" she whispered to her mother.

"If only we could!" sighed the woman, afraid even to think of such a wonderful thing. Her life had been one of constant movement and re-adjustment, from one hostile environment to another. This place was like something she had seen in a dream, and the people were warm and kind and happy in a way she had never known before.

She relaxed under their kindness very quickly, but for her husband it was more difficult. He had been trained to suspicion and resentment so long that to trust people did not come easily to him.

Although Isar was anxious to return to his own home he was persuaded to rest a day or two amongst the friendly villagers. He had been through a great deal and they could see that he was not really fit enough to make the journey.

His protests were soon silenced and Lark prepared a comfortable sleeping place for him in one of the houses.

Her face was the last thing he saw as he fell wearily and heavily to sleep, and the first that greeted him at the dawn.

She held fresh spring water for him to drink and warm barley bread for him to eat.

Later they walked through the flowering grass and found a small and secluded valley full of ferns and trees and running water.

They sat long and silently on a mossy rock and thought about the things that they had endured together since they had met, the terror of the hunt, the days in the dark palace of Na-Groth and the violence of his final overthrow.

Isar wanted to tell Lark of his gratitude for how she had saved his life more than once. He wanted to tell her how he felt when he was with her. He wanted to tell her how he felt about her, and how he hated to think of their parting . . . but the words would not come.

His heart was full of unsaid things.

He looked helplessly at her, thinking of the irony that it was he who had the tongue and could not use it, and she who was dumb and yet could communicate in deep and subtle ways.

The sunlight shafted through the leaves onto her soft and shining hair. Her thin face had colour in it now, and her eyes were the most beautiful he had ever seen.

Before he knew what he was doing he was leaning

forward and his lips were on hers, his arms close about her.

"I love you," his heart was saying, "I love you and I cannot help myself!"

In that kiss the whole world seemed to dissolve and disappear, and when he at last emerged from it, it was as though it were a new day.

He held her at arm's length and looked at her with amazement.

How had this happened?

How had he allowed it to happen?

She was smiling, but it was the saddest smile he had ever seen.

He knew that she loved him and that it was forever— . . . but . . . the sadness of her smile reminded him that he was not free to love anyone but Deva . . . and Deva had not been in his thoughts for a long time.

He dropped his hands from her arms, feeling the longing to hold her close again.

He turned away.

He tried to force the world to be as it had been before he came to Klad.

But he knew that this was not possible, nor what he wanted.

Lark stood up and moved across the stream and away down the valley.

When she was out of sight he buried his face in his hands and tried to think of Deva.

Berka's insistence that this was the place she wanted to live, won her father over at last.

He asked permission of the villagers and was granted it.

They began to choose the wood and start the preparations for building their home. It was to be sturdy like the other village houses, and not make-shift like the temporary shacks on Na-Groth's plain.

Berka was already looking better and had adopted Gerd, as she had adopted Gya, as her special charge. They had a really good relationship, though people listening in to their conversations, might not have guessed it.

"Are you going to sit all the time feeling sad?" she said to him sharply one day.

"No, I am going to become a messenger and run between the Temple and Klad every full moon," he answered sarcastically, his eyes sparking with resentment.

"Well, you cannot run sitting down in a chair!"

"Perhaps I will fly!"

"You *could* fly, but you will be too soft, like the milk and the soup your mother brings to you."

"I suppose you expect me to get up and fetch my own food?"

"Yes," said Berka.

Gerd glared at her.

His legs had both been damaged and there was no way one of them would ever work again. Possibly his left leg could take some weight and would heal after a time.

Did this fool girl not realize what he was going

through? Did she think he *enjoyed* being waited on and watching everyone else doing the things he wanted to do?

"If Spear-lord Karne can make a frame for flying, we can make a frame for walking," she said boldly. "You will see!"

He looked at her sceptically, but there was a glimmer of hope in his mind.

He insisted on being left alone for a long time after this and when he did permit anyone to come near him, it was Berka.

"Fetch me these things," he said preemptorily.

"Aha!" said Berka triumphantly, "the frame for walking!"

Gladly she worked to gather all the bits and pieces together, and patiently worked with him to construct the frame.

When it was finished it was cumbersome and difficult to move.

It was on her suggestions that he eliminated certain of the rods and simplified the whole thing until it was light and practical.

It was still painful for him to put any weight at all upon his left leg, but he was determined to sit no more and grow soft "like milk and soup."

Berka had the sense to guess that he must not overdo it at first, and supervised short, secret practice sessions until the leg became gradually better.

"It will be much surprise for everyone. When we can do it properly we will walk amongst all the people and show them how clever we are!"

"We?" Gerd asked raising his eyebrows.

Berka laughed and shrugged.

She identified so much with his struggles that she almost believed they were her own.

His appearance at the next festival of the Full Moon, walking with his frame, caused a sensation.

After Gerd's village most of Isar's party made straight for home, but Isar and Lark took a detour to visit Gya's mother and sisters. They were thrilled with the news of his part in Na-Groth's downfall and proud of his work with Karne in rebuilding the stricken country.

They persuaded Isar and Lark to delay their journey a few days longer, and made them very welcome.

The two young people had tacitly agreed that nothing could come of their love for each other, but they were still loath to come to the moment of parting. They decided to stay and help the village in any way they could to re-establish the sanctity of their Sacred Circle.

The bodies of the people who had been murdered in the Circle were gently removed at last by a group of the older men.

The ancient burial ceremonies were performed, and their families allowed the healing dignity of prayer.

Up to this time no one had dared approach the Circle, so effective had Na-Groth's spell of terror been. Isar himself had felt it on his first visit, and even now it took great courage to enter the place.

Having buried their dead the villagers were at a loss to know what the next move should be.

Isar promised that the Temple would send a priest who would cleanse the Tall Stones properly. Until that time they should pray as best they could from their own hearts.

Lark behaved strangely near the Circle as though she could hear something the others could not hear.

Isar who had been beside her let her go and, as though in trance, she walked between the ancient megaliths and stood with her eyes closed in the very centre.

"It is still a place of evil," Gya's mother whispered anxiously. "Who knows what wraith of darkness might possess her?"

Isar took a step forward anxious to protect her, but when he came to take her hand the strength he received from her touch amazed him. It was as though together they made one Being, but that Being was greater than the both of them.

Words that were not his own began to issue from his mouth.

"This Circle is sacred to the Lord of Life and is held until his coming.

"Within it let no man stand who is not prepared to meet him face to face."

He tried to move but his limbs were as heavy as stone.

Before him stood a man, beautiful with age, smiling into his eyes.

"I have kept my promise, and now I am needed elsewhere."

Isar longed to talk with him so wise and gentle was his face but even as he reached forward with his longing, the figure began to fade and disappear.

He found himself looking into Lark's eyes and she was smiling.

She led him out of the Circle, and when they looked back, they could see the dark shadow of Groth was no more upon it.

It was Vann's suggestion that Deva be given a sleeping potion.

"She has suffered great strain over these troubled times and her mind is confused and tired. Deep rest is what she needs."

Kyra's face was haggard and pale.

She could see her daughter through the half open hangings of the inner chamber, decking herself out in her finest clothes. She had insisted on rising in spite of their warnings, claiming that her Lord Groth was waiting for her and she must dress in a way befitting her new station in life.

There was a hard, brittle arrogance about her now that did not suit her, and her eyes were as cold and blank as polished jet.

She spoke with an authority that they found hard to disobey. She seemed indeed the queen of Groth.

Khu-ren was summoned, but he was too busy to come

at once and so Kyra and Vann made the decision by themselves.

The potion Vann prepared carried the danger of death, but if it did not kill, it certainly healed minds afflicted with strange and disturbing fantasies.

"My lady," called Deva, harshly snapping her fingers, "pass me your collar!"

She was referring to the beautiful deep collar of beaten gold in the shape of a sickle moon, that Kyra wore for thanksgiving festivals.

Kyra's hand went to her throat protectively.

"Give!" commanded Deva, moving forward menacingly.

Her mother looked into her eyes and was shocked at the ferocity she saw there.

She looked at Vann and gave an almost imperceptible nod.

Vann left the chamber quietly.

The priest of the Sun unclasped the shining collar and held it out to the stranger that stood before her.

"Put it on," commanded Deva, turning and presenting her neck to her mother as though she were mistress and Kyra were her slave.

Silently Kyra obeyed and fastened the sun metal about the girl's throat.

The new queen of Groth then held out her arms and her mother transferred the long, coiled bracelets of gold from her own arms.

"The ear-rings as well," said Deva coldly.

Gold ear-rings were threaded through her lobes.

She stood very proud and tall beside Kyra, the robe of black wool flowing to the floor, the gold that had shone so warmly on the older woman's form, now glinting with a different kind of light.

"She is possessed," thought Kyra, and remembered the queen of Na-Groth. "Is it possible?"

At this moment Vann returned with three small cups of beaten gold.

"Here is honey wine," he said. "Let us drink to your new lord."

Smiling with a falseness that Deva would have suspected had she been more herself, he presented both women with a cup and retained one for himself.

Deva for the first time showed a touch of graciousness as she took the honey wine.

She was pleased that they were beginning to accept her in her new role.

"Let us drink to my lord," Deva said, and raised her cup.

Vann and Kyra put the wine to their lips but did not drink.

Deva drained every drop.

There were tears in Kyra's eyes as they lifted the child and carried her to bed.

Gently she removed the gold collar from her throat, the bracelets and the ear-rings.

Gently she covered her with fine fur rugs.

"Sleep well, my child," she whispered. "Wake well!"

"She will be all right, my lady," Vann said. "I did not give her much."

Kyra could have fallen where she stood she was so tired.

"You too must sleep," Vann said.

Kyra smiled wanly.

"But not with your special wine."

"No, not with my special wine."

When Lark and Isar reached Lark's home village they were horrified to find nothing but the burnt remains of the houses, broken and charred cooking pots and a few battered remnants of once cherished possessions.

Lark ran from house to house weeping, and Isar stood aside, his heart feeling her sorrow, but not knowing where to begin to comfort her.

"Perhaps they are not dead," he said at last. "It is possible they were taken as slaves."

Lark stood still a while and looked at him, thinking about what he had said.

It was possible.

But in the centre of the village they found an untidy mound of earth and under it they found the bodies of the villagers, many of them badly mutilated.

Isar led her away, but she pulled at his arm and tried to make him turn back.

"What is it now?" he asked gently, wishing, as he had wished so many times, that she could talk.

She pointed back to the mound, her eyes swimming in tears.

There was something that needed doing.

She would not leave until it was done.

He thought he understood.

Her friends and family had died by violence and had had no proper burial.

They gathered all the pebbles they could find and piled them upon the mound, building it higher and higher until it was a cairn that could be seen for a long, long way.

With each stone Isar murmured a short prayer for their safe journey in the many realms that are beyond this one.

Each stone became charged with love and caring.

Each stone would mark a man's life ended, and a man's life begun.

When it was done Isar took Lark's hand and they walked together away from her home.

"You have no home now. No people. You must come with me. My people will be your people."

Lark hung her head.

All the strength she had had in the testing moments of crisis seemed to have deserted her. She looked very young and frail and lost.

"There is no other way," Isar said gently.

She looked at him and her eyes were full of sorrows.

"I know . . . I know, my love . . . there is Deva . . . but . . . I cannot, no, I will not, leave you here. Kyra will take you to her heart and will tell us what is best to do . . ."

At the mention of Kyra a faint flicker of light came to Lark's eyes and she seemed to make a decision. Was this not the name the beautiful old man of her visions had spoken?

She picked up the carrying pouch she had let fall upon the ground, slung it over her shoulder and walked eastward with Isar.

Deva slept long, deeply and apparently peacefully, but the priest of dreams, Lea, could tell as she looked down upon the girl that she was undergoing a difficult and dangerous experience.

She had returned yet again to her ancient homeland, but had found this time that the garden she had loved was gone and the wind moaned softly and stirred the sand over the cracked white paving stones. The fountain was dried up, the lilies long since dead.

The grand palace where she had lived was ruined, desert birds nested in its broken walls, and lizards were the only attendants in the king's chamber.

"Father!" she cried, rushing from desolate room to desolate room. The empty corridors echoed back her call.

She saw her name engraved upon a stone and fell weeping beside it. There was no doubt this was the place of her childhood. Had she not watched the name being carved?

How was it that she turned her back and all that she had known had fallen so to dust?

"Father," she wept, "I need you. Help me."

Across the dead, hot sands of the desert she could see the strange pyramidal shapes that her father had

ordered to be built. There were more than she remembered and some were dazzling white with caps of gold.

Even as she saw them, she was beside them, and
they towered above her.

They were not quite as she remembered them in her
father's day, but his genius had created them and his
teaching was in them.

She looked around.

How strangely empty the place was.

She remembered it full of sweating slaves and
shouting overseers, full of stone masons hammering
. . . men talking and calling . . .

How strangely quiet.

It was as though she were the last person left on
earth.

She shuddered and looked around for shelter from
the terrible brilliance of the sun.

On the eastern side of one of the pyramids was a
shaded colonnade leading to a door.

She walked down it, her eyes fixed on the solid stone
slab.

She read the inscription.

"Enter not here if you have anything to hide.

For here is nothing hidden."

The door opened even as she read the words and she
was in the icy darkness of the interior.

There was no light, but she could see.

Shivering, she walked forward, knowing that there
was no way back.

The door had closed behind her, and the hollow, reverberating sound of its closing would be with her for the rest of time.

The narrow passage led deeper and deeper into the building.

From time to time she reached a small chamber and then found herself leaving it by a passage narrower and lower than the last.

The first few chambers were full of beautiful things, vases and furniture and clothes, the walls covered with rich and skilful paintings.

She looked about her and saw her former life depicted on the walls, even to a representation of her favourite garden with the fountain and the lilies.

She longed to stay, but when she touched the lilies they were cold and hard, and the water could not quench her thirst.

The next chamber seemed to represent her life in the green northern country where she had lived long ago with Isar.

Joyously she rushed to him as he sat upon his throne, but as she touched him he fell to dust, and she screamed, her scream causing the dust of millennia to fall from the ceiling and the walls.

She could not leave the chamber fast enough.

The corridor became darker and narrower.

The next chamber was featureless and blank.

And so was the next.

Deeper she went, and every chamber she came to was bare and black.

She knew these were the lives she had refused to have and she was filled with regret.

"If I had my time again," she whispered with a dry mouth. "If *only* I could have my time again!"

She was on hands and knees now crawling along the rough stone tunnel, with scarcely enough room to raise her head to see whether another chamber was to come.

"Will I reach the centre and find that I am crushed like an olive in an olive press? Will the stone close over me and I be trapped here forever?"

The pain of the pounding of her heart was almost too much to bear.

If she had wanted to turn back now there was no way she could have manoeuvred the turn in that small space.

She had to go on.

There was another chamber.

It was enormous, opening before her like a giant cavern.

She straightened her cramped limbs and dragged herself to her feet, staring about her with awe.

It was a sombre and impressive place . . . contrast of blackness and fire . . . harsh light and deathly darkness.

The shadows in the corners held dreadful mysteries.

In the centre, on a throne of swords, sat a figure as fearful as she had ever imagined.

Eyes like holes over nothingness.

A mouth that was the door of Dread.

"My lord!" she cried and fell upon her knees.

This must be Groth and she had been brought to his palace to be his queen.

He lifted a scaly hand and pointed at her.

She felt a searing pain in her forehead and light seemed to explode in her head.

"Choose!"

A voice roared in her ears.

"Choose!"

She shut her eyes.

She shut her ears with her trembling, icy hands.

She turned and ran.

The corridor was larger than it had been and admitted her full and running figure.

Back through the darkness she fled.

Back through the silent, empty chambers.

Through the chambers of her past.

Through the chambers of her mistakes.

"I choose!" she screamed.

"I choose!

"Kyra, my lady," she shrieked, "Lord of Light, save me!"

The stoney door fell open.

The sunlight burst into fragments and whirled around her. She saw Kyra standing beside her, holding a lily.

"Welcome home, my child," she said, and her smile was the most beautiful thing that Deva had ever seen.

Sobbing she flung herself into her mother's arms and Kyra took her.

Khu-ren, Lea and Vann looked at each other, smiled, and quickly withdrew.

News of the approach of Isar and Lark travelled ahead of them and Fern, Kyra and Deva set off to meet them.

Since she had recovered from her "illness" Deva had been very quiet and thoughtful. Gradually the colour had come back to her cheeks and the softness back to her eyes. She played with Fern's youngest child and laughed with almost as much carefree abandon as she used to have.

But Kyra could see that she had changed.

She was older, and there was something that needed settling still in her heart.

Strangely she did not seem impatient for Isar's return any more, and when she received the news that they were going out to meet him, she hesitated about joining them.

"What is the matter?" Kyra asked, seeing the look in her eyes.

"Nothing," Deva said.

Kyra enquired no further.

Deva was a woman now and must be allowed the dignity of solving her own problems.

At the last minute she decided to join her mother and Fern. Kyra noticed that she dressed and groomed herself very carefully.

"You look nervous," she ventured to say.

But Deva did not reply.

They met Isar and Lark in a wood.

Fern was the first to reach him and she fairly smothered him with kisses. He lifted her off the ground and swung her round in his arms.

Laughing she saw the green trees whirling and the sky dancing at his return.

"I think I could burst with happiness!" she cried.

He kissed her lips, her eyes, her hair, and put her down.

Above her head he met the eyes of Deva.

He would have expected her to be the one to fling herself at him.

She seemed different, more dignified.

Lark watched him as he walked towards her.

He stood in front of her, looking down into those beautiful dark almond eyes he remembered so well.

The two Beings who had known each other through millennia knew that a subtle change had taken place in each other and in their relationship.

Everything had gone quiet around them.

Fern and Kyra and Lark moved not a muscle.

He looked his question.

Deva stepped forward and kissed him softly on one cheek and then the other.

"Welcome home," she said quietly.

Was this the impetuous, possessive child he had left behind?

"You and I, my lord," she said now, holding her head high and speaking steadily . . . only Kyra could see that her hands were trembling and that she was clenching and unclenching them behind the folds of her

dress . . . "You and I have much to tell each other.
Will you walk with me?"

Isar looked swiftly at Lark.

Deva did not miss the look.

Lark's eyes were masked.

This was between Isar and Deva, and she would not
interfere though her heart might break with the strain
of holding back.

Isar then turned to Kyra.

Imperceptibly she nodded.

Slowly the two walked away from the others down a
green tunnel of leaves.

They walked close, but they did not touch.

They had gone a long way before either of them
spoke, and then it was Isar who stopped walking and
prepared to tell what was in his heart.

"No," Deva said, holding up her small hand, "let me
speak while I have the courage.

"You have been away a long time, how long I cannot measure by the fullness and the waning of the
moon, the cycles of the sun. I only know that during
that time whole peoples have lived and died, buildings
of stone have risen and fallen, wind and sand have covered the places we once loved."

Isar was listening attentively, his face deeply
thoughtful. He did not remember the ancient times as
well as Deva did.

"Our paths must separate, my lord. I know this now,
though the pain of accepting it is still with me.

"I will never be myself, know myself, grow as a

Being should, if I hold always to what I was and what I had.

"All this life as Deva I have felt unsettled, a stranger amongst strangers, not knowing where I belonged. I have done foolish, wicked things . . .

"No, do not speak.

"I know what I have done and what I have been.

"Someday I will tell you of the vision that made me see myself . . . but not now . . .

"O Isar . . ."

Her voice broke.

"I will love you always . . . but . . . not as I have done."

She stopped speaking and the gentle forest noises of rustling leaves and bird calls took over.

The young man stood, torn between two loves, the one he had grown accustomed to having, and the other whose love was new and full of mystery.

Deeply they looked into each other and the valediction they spoke was wordless.

Deva suddenly shook herself and something of the old mischievous spark came back to her.

"Come," she said briskly, "I will race you back to the others!"

Before he could turn his mood around she was off over the crackling twigs, sunlight flickering on her flying hair.

He was soon level with her in spite of her having started before him, and he should have been warned by the old fiery glint in her eye.

Quick as the lash of a lizard's tail her dainty foot shot out and tripped him up.

Laughing she was off again and he was left struggling in a bed of leaves and soft mud.

In the time that followed many changes took place.

Lark moved into the house of Lea next to the Temple and the priest who had no daughter of her own took her to her heart.

Isar told Lark all that had passed between Deva and himself, and they did not immediately think of marriage between themselves.

Lark could feel he wanted time between the new life and the old, and she knew also that he was still concerned about Deva and anxious not to hurt her in any way.

But as time went by and Deva seemed to return to her old teasing, volatile self, loving towards him but more as a sister than as a lover, they began to relax and meet sometimes.

Isar found more and more that they did not need to use words between them. He seemed to have such closeness with Lark that her thoughts could blossom in his mind as though they naturally grew there.

To speak with others she developed a language of hand signs which he knew how to interpret.

Kyra was told of the old man in Lark's vision and tears came to her eyes.

Maal indeed had kept his promise, but Kyra was still lonely for him.

Later there was great rejoicing when Karne returned in triumph, a great collar of beaten gold about his neck, a cape of woven cloth flowing from it, and the handsome Gya at his side.

The wedding of Lark and Isar was quiet and gentle.

That of Deva and Gya was full of noise and merriment, the gayest one the Temple community had ever seen.

MASTER NOVELISTS

CHESAPEAKE CB 24163 $3.95
by James A. Michener

An enthralling historical saga. It gives the account of different generations and races of American families who struggled, invented, endured and triumphed on Maryland's Chesapeake Bay. It is the first work of fiction in ten years to be first on *The New York Times Best Seller List*.

THE BEST PLACE TO BE PB 04024 $2.50
by Helen Van Slyke

Sheila Callaghan's husband suddenly died, her children are grown, independent and troubled, the men she meets expect an easy kind of woman. Is there a place of comfort? a place for strength against an aching void? A novel for every woman who has ever loved.

ONE FEARFUL YELLOW EYE GB 14146 $1.95
by John D. MacDonald

Dr. Fortner Geis relinquishes $600,000 to someone that no one knows. Who knows his reasons? There is a history of threats which Travis McGee exposes. But why does the full explanation live behind the eerie yellow eye of a mutilated corpse?

8002